Also by Kate Sedley

Death and the Chapman

Available from HarperPaperbacks

The Plymouth Cloak

The Second Tale of Roger the Chapman

KATE SEDLEY

HarperPaperbacks

A Division of HarperCollins Publishers

HarperPaperbacks *A Division of* HarperCollins*Publishers*
10 East 53rd Street, New York, N.Y. 10022

A hardcover edition of this book was published in 1993
by St. Martin's Press.

Cover illustration by Michael Storrings

First HarperPaperbacks printing: November 1994

Printed in the United States of America

HarperPaperbacks and colophon are trademarks of
HarperCollins*Publishers*

10 9 8 7 6 5 4 3 2 1

PROLOGUE

With some part of my mind, I knew that I was still asleep. I could feel the roughness of the hard stone floor on which I lay; the bundle of hay which served me as a pillow tickled my cheek; the coarse grey blanket, provided by the Hospitallers of St. Cross rubbed against my cheek. At the same time, my dream was very real; so real that I could feel the wind in my face as it soughed through the branches of the trees which arched and interlaced above me; feel the unevenness of the path beneath my feet; hear the scufflings of some small nocturnal animal as it hurried to safety among the tangle of briers and bushes which bordered the track.

I also knew that I was afraid, although of what I was as yet unsure. Apprehension was turning to fear as I padded slowly forward, my boots making no sound on the soft, damp earth, except for the occasional snapping of a twig. If I raised my eyes, I could now and then glimpse the crescent moon, riding cold and high between the clouds. Below me, every once in a while, where the bank dropped sheer and the bushes thinned, I could see the glint of water. Once or twice I hesitated, glancing back over my shoulder as though listening for something or someone, and at these moments I was divorced from my body, a watcher in the shelter of the trees. But almost immediately I was myself again, seeing with my own eyes, my ears straining after every sound, conscious of the prickle of sweat across my shoulder-blades.

I descended slowly, stopping at each twist and bend of the path, scanning the darkness ahead, looking anxiously for something, yet scared of finding it. An owl swooped low across my line of vision, gliding silently from one perch to another. The sudden movement startled me, and I stood stock-still, my breath coming short and fast, my heart pounding in my breast. Then, carefully, I resumed my walk, aware that I had nearly completed my descent and was standing on a level with the river. For as the path flattened out and the trees drew back, I was able to see the broad expanse of water stretching to the farther bank, silvered fleetingly with moonlight.

I prowled warily forward, the tall grasses which fringed my side of the river reaching half way up my legs. The owl hooted in the trees behind me. Suddenly, the toe of my left boot stubbed against something; some large object lying half hidden among the vegetation. The hairs on the nape of my neck rose, and I knew that I had stumbled on whatever it was I had been so fearful of discovering. I glanced down just as the moon appeared once more from behind the clouds, and I could make out the shape of a body. Whose body it was I had no idea, whether man or woman, young or old; although through the clinging mists of my dream, I somehow knew that I already had this knowledge. I stopped and, overcoming my reluctance, peered more closely.

The person was lying face down. I put out a hand to

touch the back of the head, then withdrew it quickly. I felt the wet stickiness on my fingers which could only mean blood. The back of the skull had been beaten in, and whoever it was, was dead . . .

The scene dissolved around me, and I was lying in a state of sweat and panic on the floor of the almshouse of the Hospital of St. Cross in Winchester, where I had been given asylum for the night.

CHAPTER

1

 It was a beautiful morning of warm autumnal sunshine, a crystal bowl overflowing at the brim; the Grail spilling its light and colour in a profusion of splendour. People were abroad early about their business, making the most of what might well be the last of the year's fine weather. For as I came within sight of the city of Exeter, it was already the last day of September in that year of Our Lord, 1473.

So far, it had been an uneasy year. As I humped my chapman's pack and plied my trade along the south coast of England, to London and back again, the towns and villages through which I passed had been rife with rumours of an impending invasion. It seemed that the exiled Lancastrians were stirring, beginning to take heart once more after their defeat at Tewkesbury two years previously. One might have thought, with King Henry and his son both dead, that the focus of their disaffection had vanished; but they had transferred their loyalty to young Henry Tudor, who was now living at the court of Brittany with his uncle

Jasper, as a guest of Duke Francis. To most people, Henry was something of a joke, his claim to the English throne not to be taken seriously, descended as he was through the bastard line of John of Gaunt. It demonstrated more clearly than anything else could have done the desperation of the remaining adherents of the House of Lancaster to find a new leader. Nevertheless, there were sufficient opponents of King Edward, old enemies and new ones, too, who had foregathered across the Channel bent on stirring up trouble.

Chief among these was John de Vere, Earl of Oxford, a man wholly committed to the Lancastrian cause; a man who had resisted all the blandishments, persuasions and bribes of King Edward to turn his coat and embrace that of the House of York; a man who preferred exile and hardship to soft living and a place at court if it involved him in what he regarded as an act of betrayal. His loyalty to Lancaster had never wavered, and I could not but admire him for it. But there were others rumoured to be involved in the current unrest who owed much to King Edward and who were at present living on his bounty, high in his favour and esteem.

One of the two names whispered most often in the alehouses and taverns along the south coast in the late winter and early part of the spring was that of George Neville, Archbishop of York, whose elder brother, the mighty Earl of Warwick, had died fighting against King Edward two years previously at the battle of Barnet Field. His complicity in whatever plot was hatching seemed to have been proved to the King's satisfaction when, in April, he was arrested and imprisoned in the Fortress of Hammes, outside Calais. Two weeks later the Earl of Oxford had led an invasion of the Essex coast, only to be severely repulsed.

The other name frequently mentioned in the same

breath as the words "treason" and "treachery" was that of the King's own brother, George, Duke of Clarence.

My approach to Exeter on that beautiful morning was through the West Gate, my travels having taken me across country from Honiton to Crediton before turning south-east to try my luck in the city. Takings had been poor the last few weeks, people, particularly the women, being un-settled by all the talk of invasion. I have noticed many times in my life that when folk are uneasy or uncertain, they hoard money rather than spend it, as though the feel of the coins in their hands, or the thought of it stored away in jars or a hole in the ground, gives them comfort; a bulwark, a talisman against mischance. Certainly country-dwellers tend to be of that disposition, but people who live in cities are less cautious. So, as I crossed the River Exe, watching the sunlight sparkle on the water, I was hoping for an upturn in my fortunes.

My spirits insensibly rose at the sight of the bustling streets, of so many people going about their business as though there were no impending threat of invasion, as if the Earl of Oxford and his fleet were not even now patrol-ling the Channel. I had been in the city once before and knew its hub to be the Cathedral Church of St. Peter. Con-sequently, I made my way along the old Roman road which was Exeter's main street and turned down an alley near St. Martin's church, which stood in a corner of the Close. As I began looking for a place to set out my wares, I could hear the day's third office being chanted inside the Cathedral and was, as always, sharply reminded of the time when I, too, would have participated in the service. But I had chosen to return to the secular life before taking those final vows which would have made me a member of the Benedictine Order. Even now, after the passage of several years, I still felt a sense of guilt at having gone against my dead mother's wishes. I comforted myself with the thought that had I not done so, two cold-blooded murderers might never have been exposed and brought to justice. I felt that by that action—undertaken at some grave risk to my personal safety—I had made my peace with God and paid the debt that I owed Him. But every now and then I had the uneasy feeling that maybe God had other ideas; that He had not yet finished with me.

That sense of foreboding was particularly strong this morning as I paused outside the Annivellars' House and took stock of my surroundings. As I did so, I became aware that there was more of a bustle, more of a thrusting sense of self-importance among some of the passers-by, than was warranted even by such a thriving and industrious town as Exeter. Then I noticed the presence of the blue-and-murrey livery worn by the retainers of both King Edward and his youngest brother, the Duke of Gloucester. As it was unlikely that the King could be in the city without a great deal more pomp and pageantry than was immediately apparent, I concluded that it must be my lord of Gloucester who, when last heard of, had been rumoured to be arraying his Yorkshire levies with a view to leading them south, presumably as an added bulwark against invasion. But what, I wondered, could possibly be the reason for his being in Exeter this bright September morning?

My curiosity was to be satisfied in a far more dramatic manner than I could have imagined. Coming to the conclusion that there was nowhere in the Close where I could comfortably display the contents of my pack, I reluctantly decided that I had no option but to start knocking on doors and speaking to the goodwife of each household. There was always the chance that, during my travels, I might have picked up some small luxuries not readily available even in the shops and market-stalls of Exeter. But first, a mazer of ale would not come amiss, and with it I might also hear some of the local gossip. Consequently, I made my way towards Bevys Tavern which stood cheek by jowl with the Annivellars' House opposite the Cathedral. I was within spitting distance of the open doorway when my left arm was clutched, none too gently, from behind and a voice spoke breathlessly in my ear.

"Roger Chapman, you're to come with me. Now. To the Duke of Gloucester. My master is in urgent need of a man whom he can trust."

Those of you who have bothered to read my reminiscences thus far will know that during my first adventure—which I referred to just now—I also managed, quite fortuitously, to render a very important service to His Grace, the Duke of Gloucester, as a result of which it appeared that I was now to be pressed into use to do him another. As there was no way in which I could refuse the request, even though it would impinge on time when I should be earning my livelihood, I reflected on the inadvisability of getting mixed up with one's betters in the first place. However, the damage was done, and there was nothing I could do about it now.

I recognized the man who had accosted me without difficulty. His name was Timothy Plummer, and I had once rescued him from an importunate pieman, over-anxious to sell his wares, in Cheapside, in London. It was this encounter which had subsequently led to my meeting with his master, the Duke of Gloucester, and all that that involved. I stared at him now a trifle stupidly, as though not quite sure that he were real.

"How did you know I was in Exeter?" I demanded. "I've hardly had time to get my bearings."

"I saw you as you were crossing the West Gate bridge

and went at once to His Grace. What does it matter?" he added impatiently. "The Duke wants to see you. You have no choice but to accompany me immediately."

"I'm aware of that," I answered bitterly. "I was going to buy myself a drink at Bevys Tavern. I suppose His Grace wouldn't be prepared to wait?"

Timothy Plummer drew himself up to his full height, but still failed to reach my shoulder, a fact which plainly annoyed him. But I was used to that. My size and strength have been, throughout my life, a source of irritation to others. (Not that I am as tall nowadays as I was in my youth. Age and crumbling bones have cut me down to size—physically if not mentally, my children inform me.)

"I am not prepared to wait," he retorted grandly.

"It's just that I breakfasted a long time ago," I grumbled. "And then only on a couple of barley cakes and honey which a farmer's wife was kind enough to give me."

My little man shrugged. "I can't help that." He jerked his head. "Follow me. His Grace is lodging at the Bishop's Palace. But he must leave Exeter by this afternoon. We've no time to spare."

I accepted the coupling of his name with the Duke's and fell in meekly behind him. He strutted ahead, his blue-and-murrey livery and insignia of the White Boar miraculously clearing a path through the jostling crowds. People turned their heads to stare at us, and a glimmer of commiseration entered their eyes as they rested on me. Plainly they thought I had committed some misdemeanour and was being led away for questioning. This, together with my rapidly increasing thirst and gnawing hunger, put me in a thoroughly bad mood. By the time I was shown into the presence of the Duke, I was hard pressed even to speak civilly, let alone display the deference which was his due.

All I could see was a man of my own age, almost twenty-one summers, as young and as vulnerable as I felt myself.

The Bishop's Palace at Exeter stands in the lee of the Cathedral, a red sandstone building, in sharp contrast to the pale Beer stone of the church. As I entered behind Timothy Plummer, there was no sign of Bishop John Bothe, but there was a hum of activity involving both his and the Duke's officials, whose general deportment and disdainful expressions—particularly when they deigned to glance at me—indicated the measure of their self-importance. This was totally at variance with the Duke's own courteous manners and pleasant, welcoming smile.

He had risen at my entrance from a carved armchair beside a small and rather smoky fire, and came forward to greet me. He must have noted my sour expression for his eyes twinkled and he said ruefully: "Roger the Chapman! It's a pleasure to meet you once again, although I fear you cannot feel the same way. I've dragged you from your work and you're cursing my presumption."

"Not—not at all, Your Highness," I stammered, disconcerted to find that he had read my mind so well. "It's just that . . . that I've had nothing to eat or drink since early this morning and . . ." My voice tailed away as I realized that I had said more than I had intended.

He smiled, the smile which lit up his face, dispelling its naturally sombre expression. "And that enormous frame of yours needs constant nourishment, is that it?" He turned to Timothy Plummer. "Fetch some breakfast for our friend here; whatever's available in his lordship's kitchens." He gave a sudden crow of laughter. "And knowing how our Bishops generally look after their creature comforts, there should be plenty, and in great variety." As Timothy Plummer vanished, none too pleased at being sent on this menial errand, the Duke resumed his seat by the fire, indicating that I should pull up a joint stool which stood against one wall, and sit down opposite him. When I had done so there was silence for a moment or two while we regarded one another.

I had forgotten how small and delicate-looking he was, the dark curtain of hair swinging almost to his shoulders. His mouth was thin and mobile, and a deep cleft ran between the upper lip and the wide nostrils of the straight Plantagenet nose. There were shadows round the eyes, as though he slept badly, and the chin was just a little too long and full for the true handsomeness of his big, blond, elder brothers. Yet in his lifetime, I have often heard him spoken of as the most attractive of the three, and I know women found him very good-looking. (To say as much today is akin to treason, but I shall tell the truth and hang the consequences.)

If Richard of Gloucester were delicate of body, he was steel-willed of mind, a fact attested to by his unwavering loyalty to his brother King Edward in the face of all adversity and temptation. Unlike his other brother, George of Clarence, his allegiance had never faltered, not even when it had meant giving up all hope of marrying the woman he loved. That sacrifice was now happily a thing of the past, and he and his cousin, the Lady Anne Neville, had been man and wife for eighteen months. And in some small way I had been instrumental in bringing that about.

The same thought must have been in his mind also, for he suddenly gave a rare grin and leaned forward, resting his elbows on his knees. For a brief moment we were no longer royal duke and the lowliest of commoners, but friends; two young men born on the same day—or at least so my mother always insisted—drawn together by the bonds of youth and the sharing of a past adventure. He reached out unexpectedly and clasped my hand.

"I owe you a great deal, Roger Chapman, and instead of rewarding you, I'm about to enlist your assistance yet again. But I promise that you won't go unrecompensed. You will be more than compensated for your loss of earnings over the next few days while you ride to Plymouth, and for however many days are needed until you return." My lower jaw must have dropped open in astonishment, but just at that moment, a serving-man entered bearing a laden tray, and the Duke laughed. "Eat your breakfast first and then I'll tell you why I need you." He nodded dismissal to the server, who had placed his burden on a table near the window. "Now, take your stool over there and tuck in. I'm sure there's no more than a good trencherman like yourself can manage."

The sight of food put all other considerations temporarily out of my mind. Even my anxiety about what sort of mission it was that I was being asked to undertake was swamped by my gnawing hunger. For the next quarter of an hour I worked my way steadily through a plate of boiled beef and mutton, a dish of soused herrings, oatmeal cakes and bacon, sprinkled with saffron, and half a small loaf, all of which I washed down with three or four cups of excellent ale poured from a large pitcher left on the table. As I cleared the final traces of food from around my teeth and drained the last dregs, I looked up to find the Duke regarding me with ill-concealed amusement. For a moment I was overcome with embarrassment, before deciding that frankness was my best weapon.

"I must apologize to Your Grace if my table manners are less than you are used to, but I rarely have the chance to taste food as good as this—or indeed as plentiful—and I'm afraid I allowed myself to be carried away. I assure you that I don't always eat like a pig let loose at the trough."

That made him laugh openly. "You didn't," he said. "It was a pleasure to see someone enjoying himself so much." His face grew serious. "It's easy to forget that not all people get enough food to sustain them every day. Now, bring your stool back here again, where we can talk." When I had complied, he went on: "How are things going with you? You haven't decided to change your calling?"

I shook my head. "I like the open road. I've never been happy being confined within four walls, which is why I left Glastonbury Abbey. But I've never thanked Your Highness properly for your offer of two years ago, to take me into your household. I tried to explain to your messenger as well as I could my reasons for refusing."

The Duke inclined his head. "He delivered his message faithfully. I was sorry, but I understood." His eyes strayed to the fire, which was nothing more now than a fringe of grey ash, trembling along the edge of what remained of the logs. "I, too, dislike the feeling of being caged. I go to Westminster as little as possible, and when I'm there I dream all the time of the Yorkshire moors." He turned to smile ruefully at me. "You and I are two of a kind, it seems, yet another reason why I know I can trust you. But I knew that the moment I first clapped eyes on you. With some people, I can tell instinctively. With others—" his tone grew bitter "—I shall never understand them." I guessed that he was thinking of his brother George, but I said nothing. It was not my place to do so. After a further pause he continued in his normal voice: "So! Down to business. You're naturally wondering why I've brought you here, and I must be ready to set off towards Nottingham as soon as possible." He shifted in his chair to face me more directly, and I gave him my undivided attention.

CHAPTER
2

 There was silence for perhaps ten seconds before the Duke spoke again. When he did so, his voice was a little sharper, a little more urgent.

"You understand that what I am about to tell you is of the greatest secrecy; that I trust you implicitly." He gave a faint, wintry smile. "Until Timothy Plummer mentioned to my secretary that he had seen you in Exeter earlier this morning, I was at my wits' end to know what to do. Whom to employ." He shrugged and added bitterly: "It's not easy nowadays to put faith in anyone." And I knew that he was thinking yet again of his brother George, and possibly also of that other George, his cousin, the Archbishop of York, now immured in Hammes Castle.

I said quickly: "Your Grace need have no fear. You can trust me implicitly."

"If I were not convinced of that fact I should not be talking to you. Your presence here is fortuitous, but it seems like an answer to prayer. And who knows? It may well be."

I guessed that he was probably right. God was calling in the second part of the debt I owed him for renouncing the chance to become one of his priests. I determined to have a brisk word with the Almighty; to ask Him just how long this was likely to go on, but now was neither the time nor the place. Instead I smiled, albeit with clenched teeth, and murmured: "God moves in mysterious ways, Your Highness."

The Duke glanced at me, a trifle suspiciously I thought, and then went on: "You cannot be unaware of the rumours of invasion which have been plaguing the country all spring and summer; of the fact that Duke Francis is said to be backing Henry Tudor's claim to the English throne and is ready to send a contingent of Breton ships and men to reinforce that claim. Even as we speak, the Earl of Oxford is cruising in mid-Channel, waiting for the opportunity to attack yet again somewhere along our shores." He lowered his eyes and began fiddling with his rings, slipping one of them repeatedly on and off his thumb. "Nor can you be ignorant of the fact that . . . that certain people very close to the King and myself have been implicated in this treason. In short, my brother and my cousin." There was a protracted pause, then he raised his eyes and continued more cheerfully: "However, the King and I are by no means convinced of Duke Francis's complicity in this matter. Not one of our agents, either in Brest or St. Malo, has reported seeing anything which could be construed as an invasion fleet. Nevertheless, we have decided to dispatch a messenger to Brittany with a letter for the Duke." Again he shrugged. "Its contents are of no consequence either to you or to the man selected for the task. Suffice it to say that certain assurances have been asked for and promises made. But it is vital that the letter reaches its destination safely." He rested his elbows on the arms of his chair and regarded me straitly above his clasped hands. "You are wondering what your part is in all this. Let me explain."

I was indeed wondering and, for a few brief, panic-stricken seconds, had been afraid that I was the selected messenger. But a moment of reflection soon allayed my fears. For such a mission it was necessary to employ a man who knew Brittany well and was familiar to its Duke. This could not apply to me who, at that time, had never left the country and knew nothing of life beyond seas. I muttered something indistinctly and hoped that Duke Richard would mistake it for enthusiasm.

He went on: "The man chosen by His Grace, the King, for his extremely important errand is one known to us and one whom we have used before." He unclasped his hands and got up abruptly, going to stand by the burnt-out fire, staring down into the embers. After a while, he said in a rasping tone: "His name is Philip Underdown and I do not altogether trust him. He has an unsavoury past and there-fore many enemies. My brother thinks I'm too nice, but I should prefer it if we did not have to use such people. But beggars can't be choosers, and the very nature of the work demands a certain deviousness of character not to be found among honest men." He raised his head and turned it once more in my direction. "As I said just now, there are many people who wish Philip Underdown harm, and it will be your job to ensure that he gets safely to Plymouth and see that he embarks on the ship waiting to carry him to Brit-tany."

"But . . . But why does Your Grace not send an armed escort with him?" I stuttered. "Surely your soldiers are able to provide him with better protection than I can?"

The Duke smiled faintly as he returned to his chair; a smile which gently mocked my naïvety. "And advertise to every enemy agent that here is a King's messenger going on an important mission to the Breton court? Our purpose would be divined immediately, Duke Francis forewarned and his mind poisoned against our proposals before our messenger had even set foot on Breton soil. King Louis of France would see to that, even if Jasper Tudor and his adherents failed to do so. No; the King would prefer his letter to remain a secret until it is placed in Duke Francis's own hands, when he can read its contents without bias. So I want Philip Underdown protected until he is safely aboard the *Falcon*, which will be waiting for him in Plymouth harbour the day after next. After that, your responsibility will be at an end and you may return here to collect your pack. It will be taken care of for you while you are away. You will leave this afternoon and spend the night at Buckfast Abbey, setting out again early tomorrow morning, which should allow you time enough to arrive in Plymouth before nightfall." A sudden thought struck him and he asked with some anxiety: "You can ride?"

A firm denial might have been my chance to extricate myself from a task which I was beginning to view with the deepest dismay and apprehension. But honesty, together with the feeling that God had, for some particular reason, singled me out for this mission, forced me to admit: "A little. I used to ride the plough horses when I was a lad, either with or without the ploughman's permission."

The Duke laughed. "In that case, we must find you a nice quiet mount for your journey and hope that the experience doesn't prove too painful." He rose to his feet, walked across to the door and opened it, speaking to someone outside for several minutes before coming back and sitting down again. "Now, are there any questions you wish to ask me?"

There were dozens, but the most burning was who exactly was threatening Philip Underdown? The Duke was unable to give a satisfactory answer.

"Maybe no one, or there may be several different

sources of danger, as I have already hinted. There must be many people from his past life who wish him ill, and it would be naïve to imagine that his work for my brother and myself during recent years had passed completely unnoticed. We ourselves are perfectly well aware of the identity of a number of foreign and Lancastrian agents working in this country. Some have been arrested, others left to continue with their work. That way we are able to confuse our enemies with false information." He smiled sadly. "I can tell by the expression on your face that this world of intrigue and deception is new to you. I only wish I could have left your innocence intact, but alas, I need you. I have sent for Philip Underdown and he will be here shortly, as soon as my men can rout him out from whatever tavern he is in at present." There was yet another pause, and it seemed to me that the Duke was turning something over in his mind, something of importance. But when he spoke again, all he said was: "You say you rode plough horses as a boy. Who was rich enough to employ horses rather than oxen?"

"The Bishop of Bath and Wells," I answered, venturing on a conspiratorial grin. His earlier remark about Bishops and their creature comforts emboldened me to believe he would share my wry amusement. Instead, my remark appeared to launch him on a further train of thought, and for several moments there was absolute silence between us. Finally, his eyes sought for and found mine. He rubbed the side of his nose with one long, slender finger.

"I must be honest with you, much as it goes against the grain. There is possibly another source of danger threatening Philip Underdown. He has recently been in the company of my brother, the Duke of Clarence, who . . . who believes him to be an agent of the Tudors. You see what a double game we are forced to play!" He drew a deep breath which caught in his throat. It was obvious, to me at any rate, that he was extremely fond of this difficult elder brother, in spite of all that George of Clarence had done in the way of personal enmity, treachery and betrayal. Duke Richard went on: "What I am about to say is for your ears only, to be discussed with no one. But I feel in the circumstances that it is only fair to tell you, as I am making you responsible for Philip Underdown's safety. My brother George has a secret, if one may call it that, for he is incapable of keeping anything totally to himself. Hints, innuendoes, knowing remarks all advertise to anyone interested that he knows something they do not. I have made plain to him that whatever he knows, or thinks he knows, I want no part in it; but even so, I have been unable to escape the knowledge that it concerns something to the discredit of the Queen's family. Now, the Woodvilles are very powerful, as you may well know, and have their spies and agents everywhere. There is bound to be at least one in the Duke of Clarence's household, but he is heedless of the danger and thinks himself, as the King's brother, immune to the Woodvilles' reprisals. And perhaps for now he is. But other people are not, and it is my fear that he may have imparted his knowledge—or suspicions—to Philip Underdown as a presumed agent of the Tudors. If this is so, the Queen's family will have heard about it and they, too, may be seeking to destroy him. This is speculation on my part, but I tell you so that you may be even more on your guard."

I digested this new information and came to the conclusion that it was danger from this particular source which was the real reason behind the Duke's concern for his messenger's safety. It was on the tip of my tongue to demand why he did not ask this Philip Underdown straight out if the Duke of Clarence had confided any dangerous information to him. Then I realized that he could not depend on receiving an honest answer. A man who was playing one devious game would not shrink from playing two. I sighed.

It was evident that I was going to have my work cut out protecting this shady character. I was not looking forward to the next couple of days.

The door opened and Timothy Plummer reappeared. He shot me a brief, curious glance before bowing to the Duke and announcing: "Master Philip Underdown."

The man who entered the room had all my attention, although he merely bestowed on me a quick flick of his very dark eyes. These were of that deep brown which is almost black; of a density of colour that disguises expression and makes the thoughts behind them difficult to read. His hair, thick and curling over the well-shaped head, was equally dark, his skin swarthy. He was tall and powerfully built; a man who looked more than capable of giving a good account of himself in a fight. I began to feel my part in his protection was unnecessary, until I reflected that no man can meet danger head-on and also guard his back. I rose and pulled myself up to the full extent of my own considerable height.

The Duke was completely dwarfed between us, although, strangely, I did not realize it at the time. His was the presence which still dominated the room, nor did he himself seem aware of his lack of inches.

"Philip," he said quietly, "this is an old friend of mine, Roger Chapman. He will ride with you to Plymouth and see you safely aboard the *Falcon*. If there is any trouble, he will be there to help you."

Philip Underdown's heavy eyebrows had risen at the introduction, and his mocking glance became slightly more respectful as he assessed my size and fighting capabilities. Nevertheless, his tone was dry as he asked: "You're an expert with the sword and daggers?"

The colour flooded my face. In those days I blushed easily, and with my fair skin it was impossible to conceal the fact. All the same, I answered steadily: "I've never learned the art of swordsmanship, but I'm expert with a cudgel. You have to be on the open road. Mine is downstairs with my pack, or I should be happy to give you a demonstration."

"Not in my presence, Roger," the Duke reproved gently. "But we both take your word for your proficiency. Isn't that sort of stout cudgel known as a Plymouth Cloak in this part of the country?"

"It is, Your Grace. They say that the first thing travellers do, when landing at Plymouth from abroad, is to cut themselves the biggest branch they can find from the nearest tree because of the number of rogues and cut-purses and outlaws who attack them while crossing Dartmoor."

The Duke laughed. "A fine commentary on the state of our royal highways in Devon. The old name for it was Dyvnaint—the land of the dark valleys. It seems that those dark valleys still remain and are put to good use by criminals. I must speak to my brother the King about it when an opportunity arises. Meanwhile, I trust your Plymouth Cloak is sufficient protection for you."

"Properly handled, it can crack a man's skull wide open or break his legs. Your Grace need have no fears on that score. I am well able to take care of myself."

"Good. Then I think that is all. Roger, as I have already indicated, you will leave your pack here and collect it when you return. You will both take your dinner in the Bishop's kitchen and travel this afternoon as far as Buckfast Abbey, where you will seek asylum for the night. Tomorrow, Friday, you will press on to Plymouth, and by high tide on Saturday the *Falcon* should be lying in Sutton Pool, ready to take you, Philip, on board and carry you to St. Malo." The Duke turned to me. "I should like a few moments alone with Philip. Wait in the ante-room for him. God be with you, Roger. I am once again in your debt."

I bowed and went out, closing the door carefully behind

me. A young man sat at a table in the outer room, busy with some papers. I recognized him from my visit two years before to Baynard's Castle in London as the Duke's secretary, John Kendall. He glanced up and nodded me towards a bench against one wall, before bending his head again over his work. He was dressed for travelling, ready to accompany his master on the first stage of his journey northward that afternoon. I should have liked to talk, to bring into the open some of the doubts and fears buzzing around inside my head; to have discussed the unexpected turn which my fortunes had taken. But he plainly had no wish to be disturbed, so I sat mumchance, staring down at my feet and only glancing up when the outer door opened.

At first, I thought it was a child who stood silhouetted against the bustle of the corridor beyond. Then I realized that it was a man, a dwarf, wearing the blue-and-murrey livery of the Duke of Gloucester. He was a little over three feet high and moved with the ungainliness of all his kind, the result of a body too heavy for the stunted legs. And his eyes held that sad, lost look that I have since seen in the eyes of other dwarfs; bewilderment mingled with outrage at the cruel joke played on them by Nature, making them the butt of their fellow men.

At that time, however, this was the first dwarf I had encountered at close quarters, although I had seen one or two at a distance. It was very fashionable then, and had been for some years, for the rich and well-to-do to employ the services of at least one midget in their households; to pet and pamper or kick and abuse them according to mood and fancy. These little men acted as pages, train-bearers and, on occasions, jesters. In some houses, they were treated as little more than pet dogs.

John Kendall raised his head and said irritably: "Not now, Paolo. His Grace is busy."

The dwarf broke into a spate of rapid Italian—at least, I

presumed it to be Italian because of its similarity to Latin and also because of the man's name. The secretary curbed his annoyance with an obvious effort and replied courteously in the same tongue. (I doubt if the Duke ever knowingly tolerated unkindness towards one another among his personal servants. The ones I met were all devoted to him.) The little man shrugged and was turning to go when the door to the inner room opened and Duke Richard emerged, followed closely by Philip Underdown. John Kendall and I sprang hurriedly to our feet. As I sketched an obeisance, I caught sight of Paolo's face.

He was looking not at the Duke, but beyond him, at his companion, with an expression compounded of hatred and fear. As I watched, Philip Underdown's eyes singled him out with a glance of mocking comprehension, then slid away again, as though the dwarf were of no more interest or importance than one of the late autumn flies which had entered through the open casement and were now buzzing drowsily about the room.

The Duke's eyebrows rose when he saw the dwarf, and John Kendall hastened to explain.

"Paolo wondered if Your Grace wished him to go with the advance party this afternoon, or to wait and follow with the rest of the baggage wagons tomorrow."

Duke Richard smiled affectionately at the little man. "Wait, Paolo. You would find it too tiring to come with us today." He nodded dismissal and turned once more to me, holding out his hand. "I shall not be here when you return, Roger Chapman, but you have my grateful thanks now and always. Once again, God be with you. I must go now. I am promised to dine with Bishop Bothe at eleven o'clock, so I shall leave you and Master Underdown to get better acquainted."

CHAPTER

3

John Kendall followed his master out of the room, the dwarf hard on his heels. Philip Underdown and I were left facing one another, like two wary animals unsure of their ground. Each was resentful at being saddled with the other, but we had no option in the matter and were forced to make the best of things.

Philip Underdown expressed what I was thinking. "I can't pretend I'm pleased to have you with me. You're likely to prove more a hindrance than a help as far as I can see. I'd do a damn sight better on my own. God alone knows what maggot has got into the Duke's head, but he's foisted you on to me and there's nothing I can do about it; although I don't mind telling you I tried while I was alone with him in there." His head jerked towards the inner room. "But he insists you come with me to Plymouth, so I'll have to put up with you for the next two days. Are you ready to eat again? According to His Grace, that was the remains of your breakfast I saw on the table."

"I'm always ready to eat," I answered with a cheerfulness I was far from feeling. I was no more looking forward to Philip Underdown's company than he was to mine. "According to His Grace, they're expecting us in the Bishop's kitchen. Shall we go and find it?"

When we were finally seated at a corner of one of the long tables in the outer scullery, surrounded by all the hubbub and uproar attendant upon the King's brother dining with the Bishop, I determined to take the Duke's advice and get to know my companion better. Knowing more about his past might possibly be of assistance later. As two large bowlfuls of beef stew were placed before us, I said: "The dwarf, Paolo, didn't seem to like you very much, from which I gather you two have met before."

Philip Underdown laughed, a sound without any warmth in it, and dipped a hunk of bread in the steaming broth. "Oh, we've met all right. He's the reason I was recruited into this employment in the first place." He saw my look of incomprehension and laughed again. "My brother and I were traders. We bought and sold anything that could be got cheap and disposed of it at a profit. We fought our way up from small beginnings until we had our own ship. Then our horizons widened: Ireland, Italy, France, Brittany. I've made a small fortune in my time— and lost it. Drink. Gambling. And of course women." His teeth showed momentarily in a predatory grin. "Then, on that last trip home from Italy, two years ago, we were attacked by pirates off the Corsican coast. My brother was killed and the vessel badly damaged. I managed to make it back to these shores and up the Channel to London, but I knew the old *Speedwell* would never go to sea again, so I paid off the crew and set about selling the cargo as quickly and as profitably as I could, with the prospect of having to start from scratch once more."

A scullion, detailed to wait on us, and only too pleased

to have a brief respite from washing his greasy pots and pans, placed two mazers of ale in front of us, managing to slop most of the liquid on the table. He withdrew hurriedly before we could complain. I stared after his retreating back without really seeing it. "But what's all that got to do with the dwarf?" I queried.

Philip Underdown sucked his teeth. "He was part of the cargo."

It was a moment or two before his words sank in, then I exclaimed in horror: "You were a slaver!" I knew also why his accent was familiar to me. He came from Bristol, and the people of that city have been involved in slavery for centuries, trading mostly with their neighbours in southern Ireland. There is a story, often repeated in my part of the world, that long, long ago, King John complained that there were more Bristolians to be found in Dublin than Irishmen; people sold by their own families as servants.

My companion looked at me with cold amusement. "I bought and sold unfortunates like Paolo. Parents and relatives of these creatures are only too willing to be rid of them, and most of them are very poor. A few shillings can make all the difference between starvation and survival. As for the midgets themselves, they often end up well clothed and fed in some noble household. What do you think Paolo's life would have been if I'd left him in Italy? Laughed at, derided, an outcast from his own kind. When I came across him, he was living with his father's pigs in their sty."

I felt confused by this argument. Instinct told me that trading in human flesh was evil, but at the same time I could see that its results might sometimes be beneficial. I mustered the only counter-argument I could think of on the spur of the moment. "But Paolo hates you."

Philip Underdown smiled scornfully and said thickly, through a mouthful of stew: "Of course he hates me. They all hated me and my brother. These creatures were our merchandise. We had no time to wet-nurse them through all the hazards of a journey, either to or from these shores. A certain amount of—what shall I say?—harshness was inevitable."

I stared at him, fascinated by a callousness which could admit so much; by his complete indifference to what anyone thought of him. Nothing I could say or do, however, would awaken in him a sense of wrongdoing, so it was pointless to try. I asked: "But why was a sea journey necessary? As you have just indicated, these mannikins exist in every country."

He shrugged and finished the remaining stew in his bowl. "Common sense. It's better to sell them in a foreign land, where they are unable to run away and return home whenever the fancy takes them. So we sold English dwarfs in Italy and France, and French and Italian dwarfs over here. At one time, there was a great demand for English dwarfs in Italy. No noble household was complete without one."

"I wonder you could find so many."

Again Philip Underdown shrugged his powerful shoulders. "There are always ways and means if one knows them. Paolo I was lucky enough to sell into the Duke of Gloucester's household. By some means or another the Duke came to hear of my history and circumstances, and suggested me to King Edward as a possible Royal Messenger. Someone who had travelled a great deal abroad and who could take care of himself. Which makes it all the more galling to have you foisted on to me for a mere two-day trip from Exeter to Plymouth. What does he think I am? An incompetent child?"

"He's taking no chances. This letter you're carrying seems to be important."

"They're all important," he retorted huffily. "Why should this one be any different?"

I wondered whether or not to broach the subject of the Duke of Clarence, but in the end decided against it. I felt I should probably get an evasive answer, and that I had asked enough questions for the time being. We had two days and nights before us, during which I might well be able to discover more. I swung both legs over the bench and stood up. "I'm ready to go if you are."

He nodded, wiped his mouth on the back of his hand and rose to his feet. "Our horses are waiting for us in the Bishop's stables. I'll show you the way."

"I must get my stick first. It's with my pack in the entrance hallway."

I duly collected it, along with my razor and a short, black-handled knife which I used for eating, knotting the two latter inside a square of stout, closely-woven woollen cloth that I happened to be carrying. Then I followed my companion out of the Palace and across the hundred or so yards to the stables.

Philip Underdown's mount was a large, fleabitten grey, a showy animal who rolled an intelligent eye in my direction, but gave, I noticed, no whinny of pleasure at the approach of his master. I was to ride a sturdy chestnut cob, to use its modern name; although in my youth those placid, good-natured creatures were known as rounceys. My few belongings went into the saddle-bag, but, as I had foreseen, the cudgel presented something of a problem. In the end I was persuaded, very reluctantly, to shorten it by several inches so that I could carry it across my saddle-bow.

"Easier to use, I should think," Philip Underdown commented. "You can take more of a swing with it. Not so unwieldy. Anyone could handle something of that size."

"You obviously know nothing of the art of cudgel-sticks," I answered tersely, restoring a little of the self-esteem which had been eroded by my clumsy mounting of the cob; an effort that had afforded much amusement to both my charge and the spotty-faced stable-boy who was assisting us. "Shall we be on our way? We want to reach Buckfast before dusk."

In fact, we had cleared the busy streets of Exeter and were moving south at a steady pace before the sun was much lower in the sky. The haze of early autumn clouded the valleys and hung over the hills like gauze. The track along which we rode was almost deserted, studded here and there with gorse bushes, the golden flowers embattled behind sharp black spikes. Mossy cushions of emerald-green indicated where rain had collected in dents and hollows of the underlying granite. The sudden bark of a raven was all that disturbed the quiet.

Mid-afternoon, we left the track, dismounted and turned the horses loose to crop the stunted grass. Philip Underdown and I sat, the sun on our faces, our backs against a convenient boulder, letting the last of the day's warmth seep into our bones. I badly needed the rest, although I would have suffered torture rather than admit it. But the truth was that every muscle and sinew of my thighs and buttocks felt as if it were being torn apart by red-hot pincers. My arms and shoulders ached with the effort of controlling even so placid a mount as mine. I leaned my head against the rock and briefly closed my eyes, watching red and orange suns roll up under my lids, thankful that my companion seemed preoccupied with thoughts of his own and disinclined to mock at my discomfort.

I have no idea what suddenly jerked me out of my doze, propelling me forward, my spine stiff with tension, my hands pressed hard down beside me on the ground; some interaction of the senses, perhaps, as when an animal scents danger. My eyes flicked swiftly from left to right, trying to locate the source of my fear. On the skyline, where the moor shelved steeply upwards, were two enormous outcrops of granite, common to that part of the world. And standing between them, clearly outlined against the rays of the dying sun, was the figure of a man . . .

I must have let out an oath because Philip Underdown, lounging beside me, his eyes half closed, sprang to his feet, his fingers already clasped about the handle of the dagger in his belt. "What is it?" he demanded.

"A man," I whispered. "Up there! Between those two piles of rocks."

I raised my hand, but when we both looked there was nothing to be seen, only the blurred distances and the sunlight striking against the granite, and the empty, silent path of turf.

Philip laughed harshly. "You're imagining things."

"There was somebody there," I protested. "I saw him as plainly as I see you." I reached for my cudgel and stood up. "Wait here. I'm going to investigate."

"And leave me all alone?" he mocked. "Is this how you obey the Duke's instructions? I might be spirited away by the fairies while you're gone."

Two could play at that game. "If you're afraid," I answered coolly, "stand with your back against the boulder, then no one can surprise you from behind. If you need me, shout. I shan't be far away."

He swore at me. "I'm coming too."

"By all means, if you're nervous at being left alone."

I did not wait for his reply, but set off across the intervening ground, taking the steep slope at a run, my aches and pains temporarily forgotten. At the top, between the two rock formations, I paused, looking cautiously around me, but there was nothing to be seen. I prowled around both outcrops, expecting at any moment to come face to face with some hired assassin, but there was no one. I glanced back to where Philip Underdown was still standing beside the horses. He shrugged and spread his arms, indicating that he, too, could see nothing. I began to wonder if the incident had indeed been a figment of my imagination.

Then, in the distance, I heard the thud of a horse's hoofs, hardly more than a faint vibration of the ground. I spun round, screwing up my eyes against the light as I peered in the opposite direction. It was difficult to see, but I thought I could just make out some movement. Then, for a few seconds, a small cloud obscured the face of the sun and a horseman was plainly visible, galloping southwards in the direction of Buckfast Abbey. I cursed under my breath, blaming myself for a tardiness of action which had allowed the man to get away. I returned to Philip Underdown.

"There was somebody there all right. I saw him riding away in the distance. I should have been quicker."

Philip shrugged. "He would have seen you coming. You wouldn't have caught him. And there's nothing to say he wasn't a perfectly innocent traveller, taking his rest as we were."

"In that case, why would he climb the tor? He would hardly have put himself to so much trouble and effort simply to take his ease. No; he was spying on us. No doubt he has been following us at a distance ever since we left Exeter."

"How did he pass us without us noticing?"

"There must be dozens of tracks on every part of this moor, which, if you know them, can be taken without detection. He was probably able to overtake us at any moment he pleased. I think we had better be moving on. We need to reach the safety of the Abbey before dusk, and it grows dark early this time of year. If there is another stranger staying at the Abbey, we shall know to be on our guard."

"I doubt if they will have many visitors at this season." Philip mounted his horse and settled himself in the saddle. "As you say, the days are getting short, and only those who have to travel are still on the roads of Dartmoor."

As I struggled to mount my own horse, still placidly eating and completely undisturbed by my clumsy efforts, it occurred to me that my companion was more shaken by what had happened than he cared to admit. The bantering, sneering tone had gone, and in its place there was an edginess which betokened strain. Philip was growing worried, whatever impression he might wish to give to the contrary. I hoped it would last. The onus of overseeing his safety would not then fall entirely to me. I prayed that the Abbey guest-house would prove to be unoccupied on our arrival. That way we could have it all to ourselves.

My prayer was not destined to be answered. As we crossed Buckfast Bridge, it became apparent that the whole vicinity of the Abbey was awash with humanity. As we passed along the village street, I reined in the cob and called to a woman leaning from an upstairs window of one of the houses.

"What's going on? We were hoping to find lodging at the Abbey, but it looks as if we may be disappointed."

"Strangers, are you?" The Devon burr was strong in her voice. "Yesterday was the Feast of St. Michael, and the Abbey has a licence to hold a fair on Brent Tor that day and the two days previous. A lot of people who came for it are still here, recovering from the effects of the Abbot's cider. Very potent stuff that be, my dear, as you'll find out soon enough if you try any. Although a great lad like you should

be able to hold his liquor." Her bold eyes slid apprecia-
tively from me to Philip Underdown. "And that goes for
you, too, my handsome."

He laughed, the worry and tension of the past hour
dropping from him as easily as a snake sloughs its skin. He
raised himself in his stirrups and, reaching up, grasped the
woman's hand, pulling her down towards him until he
could plant a resounding kiss on her cheek. She laughed
and returned it with interest.

As we pushed our way through the crowds of people, I
remarked: "She was a bit old for you, wasn't she? She had
more than a few wrinkles, and what I could see of her hair
beneath her cap was turning grey."

Philip turned his head and grinned. "When you know
me better—which Heaven forbid!—you'll discover that I
like women of all ages. A woman would have to be in her
dotage, or extremely ugly, to repel me. Thin, fat, tall,
short, young, old—I'll lay them all if they'll let me. And
most of them will."

I didn't doubt it. He was a man who took what he
wanted, without scruple; ruthless in his determination to
get his own way. Human life and dignity was cheap in his
eyes, as he had already demonstrated. I said nothing and
urged my horse forward to the Abbey gates, where one of
the lay brothers was on duty.

"We're on the King's business," I said. "My friend here
will show you his letter of credence. We need asylum for
the night."

"You and half a dozen others," he grumbled, but he let
us in without asking for any identification. "You'd best see
Father Abbot if you're who you say you are. Wait here and
I'll go and find out if he's at liberty. The guest-house is
full, but he'll accommodate you somewhere. Probably in
his own quarters."

While he bustled away, Philip and I dismounted. As I

stooped to unfasten my saddle-bag, I experienced a strong sense of being watched, but when I turned my head, everyone seemed intent on his own business. Nevertheless, the feeling persisted and my uneasiness returned.

CHAPTER
4

Abbot John Kyng was a pleasant, courteous man. At least he seemed so to me, and I cannot recall ever having heard anyone speak ill of him, although I suppose there may have been those who disliked him. At that time, in the year 1473, he had been Abbot of Buckfast for almost nine years and was to remain so for another quarter of a century. A distinguished scholar, he had formerly been Proctor of St. Bernard's College, Oxford, and had written several theological treatises which had found favour in Rome.

He rose to greet us as Philip and I entered his cell, the white Cistercian robes hanging loosely on his spare frame. "I am informed you are on the King's business and need a bed for the night."

Philip glared at me. "It is not supposed to be generally known, Father. My companion here was over-zealous in his desire to make certain of our accommodation."

I had the grace to blush. My tongue had indeed run away with me and I had forgotten the need for caution. We should of course have taken our chance with the rest of the travellers and revellers besieging the Abbey for shelter and not drawn attention to ourselves in this manner.

The Abbot, sensing my discomfiture, gave me a reassuring smile. "The lay brother who brought you to me finishes his present spell of duty at the Abbey tonight and is returning to his farmhouse at first light tomorrow. He is extremely trustworthy and keeps his own counsel. You need have no fear that he will repeat what you told him. As far as anyone else is concerned, you have delivered a message to me from Bishop Bothe, and it will therefore not be thought remarkable if I ensure you have a bed for the night. The Infirmary is unoccupied at present. I will speak to our Brother Infirmarian about your sleeping there. But it will be advisable for you to eat with our other guests. It will give you the necessary opportunity to allay any suspicions which may have been aroused by your preferential treatment. No irreparable harm has been done."

"No thanks to you," Philip hissed in my ear as we made our way to the refectory, where the monks were starting to dispense the evening meal. "I knew I'd have done better on my own."

I said nothing; partly because there was no real excuse I could offer—I had been careless and that was all there was to it—and partly because I still found it disconcerting to discover that not all churchmen felt themselves bound by the rule of strict truth. They bowed the knee to expediency far oftener than they would like you to think. I suppose I was very green in those days to have expected otherwise. We stood in line to collect our bowl of broth, slice of black bread and wedge of pale, goat's milk cheese, before going to sit down at one of the long trestle tables. To my relief, no one seemed interested in us or commented on the fact that we had been granted an interview by the Abbot, and I was forced to the conclusion then, as I have been many times since, that generally people are too wrapped up in their own concerns to be fully aware of what is going on around them.

My companion was grumbling morosely about the quality of the food and cursing the Duke's insistence that we started our journey that afternoon instead of waiting for daybreak tomorrow. "With hard riding," he added, "we could have reached Plymouth by nightfall."

"I couldn't," I retorted. "And maybe His Grace thought you were safer out of Exeter. Besides, there's nothing wrong with this broth. It's excellent."

It was fish soup, hardly surprising with the River Dart so close at hand and plentifully stocked with freshwater fish. The brothers could take their rods and lines to the banks every day.

Philip Underdown snorted but made no further comment, merely shovelling the food into his mouth as fast as possible. He was growing bad-tempered again, my presence proving a constant source of irritation to him. I decided to say as little as I could for the rest of the meal and contented myself with looking about me at my fellow diners. Most of them, as the village woman had said, were revellers left over from St. Michael's fair, recovering from the effects of too much cider. Tomorrow, they would wend their way home, north, south, east and west, to various parts of the moor, even as far afield as Plymouth or Exeter, to tell those unfortunate enough to be left behind what an enjoyable time they had had. The drunken stupor of today, the headaches, the blurred vision, would all be forgotten. There were, however, a few bona fide travellers, like ourselves: a couple of mendicant friars—Franciscans, judging by their grey habits—and a soberly dressed, middle-aged man sitting at the end of a table near us, saying nothing to his neighbours and keeping his eyes fixed on his plate. I stared at him long and hard, but there was no possible way of knowing if this was the man I had seen on the moor earlier in the day. Once, as though conscious of my scrutiny, he half turned his head and raised his eyes fleetingly to mine, but his features remained expressionless. If he had any interest in me and my companion, he gave no sign.

We had almost finished our meal, when there was a sudden commotion behind us, as of someone swearing and rising clumsily to his feet. A moment later, a hand descended on Philip Underdown's shoulder and a voice rasped, "I thought it was you!"

Philip, who was cleaning out his bowl with the last of his bread, slewed round and glanced up. The man standing over him was short and stocky, with light sandy hair and lashes, a straggling beard slightly more reddish in colour, and a leathery, weatherbeaten countenance in which the most striking feature was a pair of very bright blue eyes. His tunic of rough wool was patched and dirty, the brown faded in places nearly to white. A strip of grubby linen wound about his neck served him in place of a shirt and the hand gripping my companion's shoulder was roughened with calluses. The ferocity of his gaze was sufficient to make me flinch, but Philip Underdown, after a single brief glance, calmly resumed his supper.

"What do you want?" he demanded.

"You know damn well what I want!" The man lowered his head until it was on a level with Philip's and I could smell his sour breath. "I want what's due to me."

"You got what was due to you two years ago. I paid you off, Silas Bywater, the same as I paid off the others."

"You promised us more. You said that if we got that rotting hulk of yours safely into port, you'd give every man aboard two gold angels apiece. All we got was a shilling."

"And lucky to get that." Philip spoke roughly, his patience wearing thin. "How could I pay you more until I sold the cargo?" He was anxious now to be shot of this unwelcome acquaintance. They were beginning to attract attention. Heads were craning at adjacent tables in an attempt to see what was going on. He tried to shrug off the hand on his shoulder, but without success. "Leave me alone!"

The man addressed as Silas Bywater hissed: "You appointed a time and date and place for us to meet you, so you could give us our share of the proceeds, but you never turned up. The other poor sods decided to make the best of a bad job and went off home to Plymouth. Some of 'em even believed you hadn't been able to get rid of the cargo, but I knew you better than that. I stayed on in London awhile and made inquiries. And it was just as I thought. You'd made a nice little profit. Done very well for yourself, and then you'd vanished. You never intended paying me and the rest of the *Speedwell*'s crew any more, did you, you lying bastard?"

One of the brothers hurried across, attracted by the raised voices, his round-cheeked face pink with anxiety, his manner flustered. "Please cease this bickering immediately," he said. "Remember that you are in the House of God."

"Then get this idiot off my back," Philip protested. "The argument's none of my making. I just want to be left alone."

"I'm not going until I get what's due to me," Silas Bywater snarled. "Two years I've been dreaming of this meeting and now, quite by chance, it's here. And to think I nearly didn't come up to the fair! Don't plead poverty, either! You look prosperous enough."

"I've told you!" Philip roared, losing his temper. "You'll get nothing from me, not ever! So slink back to whatever kennel you've crawled out of and let me be!"

I decided it was time to take a hand. The little monk was making ineffectual noises and looking around him for reinforcements, but none was forthcoming. His fellows were either in their cells preparing for Compline or about their allotted tasks, and no one else seemed inclined to interfere. I swung my legs over the bench and rose slowly to my feet, pulling myself up to my full height as I did so. Reaching out, I forced Silas Bywater's hand from my companion's shoulder, gripped both his wrists and spun him round to face me.

"Leave my friend alone," I told him quietly, "or you'll have to deal with me as well."

He swore furiously and tried to free himself, but in my youth I had enormous strength in my hands. No matter how much he writhed and squirmed, I was still able to hold him without much difficulty. In the end, he had to admit defeat and stared up at me, panting from his exertions. Philip had also risen and was standing beside me, a look of such contempt on his face that I was not surprised when my captive made one last effort to break away. In his shoes, the object of such scorn, I, too, would have wanted to lash out with my fists. I tightened my grip until I heard one of his bones crack. Silas shrieked with pain and I let him go, to sink down on a bench, nursing his injured wrist and pouring forth a flood of imprecations. The little monk pressed both hands over his ears in horror.

I turned to Philip Underdown. "Let's get out of this. We're attracting too much attention. We've an early start in the morning. It's time we were asleep."

He nodded, and I gathered my black-handled knife from the table and my bundle and cudgel from beneath the bench, where I had placed them at the start of the meal. In silence, but uncomfortably aware of everyone's eyes upon us, we made our way to the refectory door. As we reached it, Silas Bywater shouted: "Don't think you've heard the last of this, Master Underdown! I know things about you that you wouldn't want made common knowledge, and don't forget that! I'll get you yet, you hell-hound!"

It was already dark and the bells were ringing from the Abbey church for the last office of the day. I should have liked to share in the brothers' worship, but I dared not leave my companion's side, and instinct told me that Philip Underdown was not a religious man. Of course, he believed in Heaven and Hell like the rest of us, but I guessed that he would have to be in *extremis* before he seriously considered the state of his soul.

"Do you know where the Infirmary is?" I inquired.

He shook his head. "No, but we can always ask."

One of the brothers, late for Compline, flapped towards us out of the gloom. In answer to our query, he pointed towards a building which stood a little apart from the others and confirmed that, at present, all the beds were empty, the aches and chills and agues of autumn not yet having begun to take their toll of the community. We thanked him, and I led the way across the courtyard. The door of the Infirmary creaked slightly as I opened it and edged inside.

The interior was very dark, and the only thing I could make out immediately was the cruciform window at the farther end. But as my eyes grew accustomed to the darkness, I could just discern the shape of a trestle, set back against the wall to the right of the doorway; and it was only a matter of moments before my groping fingers encountered what they were seeking, a rush-light in its holder and, nearby, a tinder-box. I managed to strike the flint against the steel and the tinder burst into flame. I lit the rush-light and held it aloft, its flickering, uncertain beam faintly illuminating the two rows of beds which faced each other down the length of the room. As I knew only too well, the single concession religious houses made to ill health was a thin palliasse fitted inside the wooden frame.

Philip Underdown advanced and began prodding one of these straw-filled mattresses with an air of disdain. He made no comment, however, probably reflecting that we at least had our privacy, and that the Infirmary cots were better than the floor of the Abbey guest-house, surrounded by the smells and sounds of our fellow diners. He removed his doublet and shoes, relieved himself in a corner of the room, checked the contents of the leather pouch attached to his belt and flung himself down on one of the beds, all without saying a word. I followed suit, but before lying down checked that my knife and cudgel were both to hand, and dragged the trestle across the door, which opened inwards.

My companion snorted derisively. "You're not afraid of that windbag, Silas Bywater, are you? He's all bluff and always has been. He'll do me no harm, I'll see to that. But in fact, he won't even try."

"It's not a chance I'm prepared to take," I answered, trying to adapt my bulk to the narrow frame of the bed. "The Duke trusts me to see you safely to Plymouth, and I have no intention of betraying that trust if I can help it." I had blown out the rush-light, but I did not need its pallid rays to see the sneer on Philip Underdown's face. I understood him well enough by now to know that he despised feelings such as loyalty and friendship. What he did, he did for money and for no other reason. I went on quickly: "You're familiar with these parts, then. Plymouth and its neighbourhood."

"What makes you say that?"

"Silas Bywater. You recruited him and the rest of the *Speedwell's* crew from there. Or did I misunderstand him?"

There was a slight pause before he replied: "No. My brother and I traded out of Plymouth as well as Bristol and

London. We took on a fresh crew each time, because months, perhaps even a year or more, could elapse between voyages while we assembled a full cargo. Dwarfs were the items that fetched most money, and, as you surmised, they were not always easy to find. Sometimes it meant scouring the country as far north as the Scottish Border. It would have been impractical to keep a regular crew kicking their heels all that while."

"And when you were in France or Italy? You had to keep your men idle then."

"Those trips were necessarily shorter. A matter of weeks only. We sold what we'd brought and used the money to restock the ship. If we found someone like Paolo, as we did that last time, we considered ourselves in luck, but the demand for dwarfs has never been so great in this country as it is abroad, particularly in Italy. But I've told you all this before, although God knows why! You're here to protect me, not pry into my affairs. So I suggest you hold your tongue and go to sleep."

He hunched himself sideways on his pallet, turning his back towards me. I linked my hands behind my head and stared up at the dimly-seen ceiling. I did not like Philip Underdown and there was something about him which made me uneasy. But I was tired. It had been a long day since I awoke in the shelter of someone's barn, just outside Exeter, early that morning; a day which had not gone as expected, but which had set me instead on the road to Plymouth in the company of this unpleasant man. I dropped one arm over the side of the cot and my fingers closed comfortingly around the handle of my knife, where it lay on the floor beside my cudgel. My senses were swimming and I, too, turned on my side, disposing my long limbs as best I could and nestling my shoulder into the mattress. I was almost across the borderline of sleep when my eyes, flicking open for a brief moment, informed me that there was another door at the opposite end of the Infirmary from which we had entered. There was quite likely a trestle there also, with a rush-light and tinder-box on it, and I knew I should get up and investigate, barring that door as well, if possible. But my body refused to respond when I willed it to rise. My arms and legs were still aching in every sinew and craved rest. If I were to mount that rouncey, now fed and watered and asleep in the Abbot's stables, tomorrow morning, with anything approaching cheerfulness, I had to sleep. My eyes shut obediently, and once again I headed towards the brink of unconsciousness. Philip Underdown was already snoring . . .

I have no idea what woke me, but suddenly my eyes were wide open. It was impossible to tell how long I had been asleep; long enough, fortunately, to turn on to my other side, facing in Philip Underdown's direction. Someone, a man, was standing over his sleeping form, the right arm raised, the hand holding a knife. Even in the darkness, I could see the pallid gleam of the blade.

I was out of bed before I was even conscious of what I was doing, my right arm locked about the assailant's throat, my left knee in the small of his back. He gave a kind of choking cry and dropped his knife with a clatter on to the stone floor, waking Philip, who immediately sat up, reaching for his dagger. Before he could come to my assistance, however, the man I was holding gave a sudden kick backwards with his right foot, catching me, more by luck than judgement, full in the genitals and causing me to loosen my grip. While I was doubled up in pain, he wrenched free, eluded Philip Underdown's lunging arm and fled for the open doorway at the far end of the Infirmary. A moment later the heavy door slammed to behind him and we were alone.

CHAPTER
5

Philip Underdown would have given chase, but I restrained him. It was still dark outside and there could be little hope of finding anyone with such a head start. All it would achieve would be to disturb the monks and rouse the other sleepers, drawing attention to ourselves and what had happened. He agreed reluctantly, relit the rush-light, placed it on the floor between our beds and sat down on the edge of his own cot, facing me. After a moment, he stopped and picked up the fallen knife, turning it over and over in his hands. Not once did he ask how I was, although he must have realized the pain I was suffering.

"Who was it?" he asked. "That creeping plague-spot, Silas Bywater?"

I eased myself full-length on to the mattress, propping myself up on my elbows. "I didn't get a proper look at him, but somehow I don't think so. He was too tall and too slender. More the build of that man who was watching us at supper yesterday evening. I think perhaps the Duke was right and you're in danger from . . . from people anxious to prevent this letter you're carrying reaching Duke Francis, in Brittany.'' I hesitated, then added: "And there may be others, for different reasons, who . . . who wish to see you dead."

He shrugged with every appearance of indifference, but conceded gruffly: "It seems the King's tame pet of a brother was right to appoint you my guardian, after all." He stretched and yawned. "I'm tired. I'll see if I can bar the other door and then we'll be able to sleep soundly until morning." It was the nearest a man like him would ever come to thanking me for saving his life.

There was indeed another trestle at the opposite end of the room and Philip Underdown dragged it across the doorway. Both entrances to the Infirmary were now barred, and we slept, if a trifle fitfully on my part, until the first pale shreds of daylight filtered through the slits of the window. Wearily I forced my aching limbs from bed, roused my companion, gathered our things together and went in search of the Abbey lavatorium. Here, we washed and scraped the stubble from our chins as best we could in the icy water before standing in line yet again for a bowl of thin gruel, a hunk of the previous day's bread and two oatcakes. Thanks to our cleanly habits, we were almost the last to arrive in the refectory, the only person later than ourselves being the well-dressed stranger. That he was well-dressed, I now had a chance to observe; a polite, quiet man with a long, thin face and a rather lugubrious expression, who gave the impression of being unable to say boo to a goose. But I knew from experience that such an appearance could be deceptive. I invited him to sit with us, wondering what his reaction might be, but he accepted with every indication of pleasure. I did my best to engage him in conversation, but found him unforthcoming. Apart from learning that he had spent the night in the seclusion of the Abbot's parlour, he told me little else.

Sitting opposite us were the two friars, one of whom was having trouble tearing his hunk of bread into manageable pieces. Glancing up, he asked the stranger, who was sitting immediately facing him, if he could borrow his knife. "For, as you know, my son, we are forbidden to carry them."

My new acquaintance fumbled at his belt, hesitated and looked flustered. "I'm sorry. I seem to have mislaid it. I must inquire if it has been discovered before I leave."

Philip Underdown's head turned sharply at this. "Lost your knife, have you? We found one, didn't we, Roger? Show it to the gentleman. It could be his."

I stooped down and untied the bundle at my feet, producing the knife, its blade wound round for protection with a scrap of woollen cloth torn from the square. "As you see," I said, pushing it towards the stranger, "it's a good one. It has a silver handle."

He hesitated, and I could almost feel the itch in his palm as he restrained the impulse to claim it. But: "No," he said resolutely, shaking his head, "that doesn't belong to me. Mine has a handle inlaid with enamel. You should place that in the keeping of one of the brothers. It's valuable."

"So you can reclaim it later," I thought to myself, satisfied that he was indeed the owner. I surreptitiously pressed Philip's foot with mine, and he returned the pressure with interest. "We'll see it's properly bestowed before we leave," I said aloud. "Which reminds me, we should be on our way." I swallowed the last of my ale and glanced pointedly at my companion's still full cup, then turned again to the other man. "Are you travelling south? If so, would you care to join us? Three are always greater protection than two against misfortune." I added mentally: "And we can keep you under our eye."

"Er—thank you, no. I shall be riding north-west to Tavistock. I have business there. But God be with you both. Have a safe journey."

Philip had swilled down his ale in almost one gulp, and now rose to his feet, wiping his mouth on the back of his hand. "We intend to," he answered shortly, "make no mistake about that." He inclined his head towards the two friars, who raised their hands in blessing. "I'm ready," he said to me. "Let's be going."

We made our way to the Abbot's stables, where we found our horses already fed and watered and only waiting to be saddled. When this was done, we led them into the courtyard and mounted, Philip springing up easily, myself hauling one leg painfully after the other, the injury of the past night adding itself to my other woes of stiffened thews and sinews. Philip watched impatiently, suddenly anxious to be gone and put as many miles as possible between us and the man we were both now convinced was his attacker. If we could reach Plymouth well ahead of time—for neither of us had any real doubt that he would follow us—we might be able to go to ground until tomorrow, when the *Falcon* should arrive in Sutton Pool to take Philip on board and carry him safely to Brittany.

As I settled myself as comfortably as I could in the saddle, I reflected that today must be the first of October and tomorrow was therefore my birthday. The Duke of Gloucester's also. We would both be twenty-one years old, but there the similarity ended. He was Constable and Admiral of England, Warden of the West Marches towards Scotland, Great Chamberlain and Steward of the Duchy of Lancaster beyond Trent. He was the King's strong right arm, a husband and a father. Whereas I was a humble chapman, a failed monk with no kith nor kin to call my own. Yet our paths had already crossed twice. Perhaps our lives were destined to intertwine.

My reverie was interrupted. "Are you going to sit there all day, like a stuffed chicken?" my companion demanded rudely. "For God's sake, let's be off."

I nodded and dug my heels into the rouncey's sides, but just at that moment the gate into the stableyard burst open and Silas Bywater appeared. He reached up and grabbed Philip's bridle.

"You haven't seen or heard the last of me, you know, so don't think it. Here! I've got this for you."

He was trying to push something into the other man's hand, but Philip hit him in the face, sending Silas sprawling in the dirt, jerked his horse's head around and vanished through the gateway, calling to me to follow. Before I had sufficiently gathered my wits to do so, however, Silas was on his feet again and standing at the cob's head. He raised one hand to mine, his battered features contorted with rage and hatred.

"Here, you give it to him," he said. "Tell Philip Underdown one day I'll catch up with him and then he'll be sorry. I know too much about him."

Once more I gave my horse the office to start, but as the animal moved forward, I glanced down curiously at the thing in my hand. It was a trailing plant stem, with small clusters of white flowers at intervals along its length. Being country born and bred, I recognized it immediately as a common weed of most cultivated ground, which flowered from midsummer until late into the autumn. And it was because of the arrangement of those flowers that it was known as knotgrass.

We reached Plymouth by mid-afternoon, having travelled harder and faster than the day before. In other circumstances, I would have protested and insisted on taking more rest; but with our nameless adversary probably close behind us, I did not dare, and put up with my aches and pains as best I could. I cursed that I had not asked the fellow his name, but Philip shrugged and said it would have been pointless.

"He would only have given you a false one, which he will change when he gets to Plymouth, so that any inquiries you might make will meet with no success. Forget it. We shall lie at the Turk's Head, where the landlord is a good friend of mine and will see that no one comes near us. He will bring us word, too, the moment the *Falcon* drops anchor."

With this I had to be content, and in any case conversation was necessarily limited. I was forced to concentrate on guiding my mount along the rutted Dartmoor tracks, if I were not to fall off and hinder our progress by injury. It was a beautiful day, as clear and transparent as a bubble, the October sun rimming the tors and distant uplands with fire. Occasionally we passed an isolated farm or tiny hamlet, whose turf-thatched dwellings threw black wedges of shadow across the sunlit grass. The plaintive call of a solitary bird could now and then be heard high above us. We met very few fellow travellers, and then only those coming in the opposite direction. No one overtook us; and although I kept glancing back over my shoulder, the moor remained empty of pursuers.

Of necessity, we stopped at midday to answer calls of nature and to buy bread and cheese and ale from the goodwife of a nearby cottage. While we ate and drank, sitting in the sun, our backs propped against the rough grey stone wall which surrounded the enclosure, I showed Philip Underdown the stem of knotgrass and asked him what it meant. He stared at it for a moment, then spat.

"How do I know? The man's mad and should be locked up. He tried to give it to me before I took my hand to him.

And that's what you should have done, not meekly accepted such rubbish.''

His vehemence, bordering almost on fury, told me that the knotgrass did mean something to him, something he would rather not be reminded of; but as I had little hope of discovering what that was, it was better to hold my tongue. I stared down curiously at the weed I was holding and tried to remember what, if anything, I knew of its properties. The only memory which came to mind was that of my mother seizing a stalk from my mouth when, boy-like, I had started to chew it. "Don't," she had said, "it's poisonous." But my mother had not always been correct in her knowledge. Like many country women, she had been extremely wise in some things, but also a prey to all kinds of old wives' tales, passed on from generation to generation, accruing a little more misinformation with each retelling. And I had never, either before or since, heard knotgrass spoken of as poisonous.

Suddenly, the plant was snatched from my hand as Philip tossed it away.

"I told you," he reiterated fiercely, "Silas Bywater's mad! Forget him. He won't trouble us again. I'll be gone from Plymouth before he can catch up with us. He's on foot. It'll take him all of today and much of tomorrow to get home."

"Was what he said true?" I asked. "Had you promised him and the *Speedwell*'s crew more money?"

I expected him to turn on me again, but he only shrugged and laughed.

"You'd promise the Devil your soul when you're battling up the Channel with a leaky ship in a storm. Only a fool would take you seriously." He added, cutting the conversation short: "Come on. If we go now, we can be in Plymouth in time for supper. The food at the Turk's Head is plain, but plentiful, and I'm hungry. Return the beakers to the goodwife and let's be going.''

I resented his tendency to treat me as a servant, but suppressed my anger. The Duke trusted me to see that his letter got safely to Brittany and that was all that mattered.

We reached Plymouth just in time for supper. The fourth hour of the afternoon was being cried as we entered at one of the gates. The town has no walls, its only danger coming from sea-borne invasion, of which there has been much in the past hundred years. But the four main roads converging on the place all led to gateways with short stockades on either side, so that people entering and leaving can be noted by the porters, and undesirable elements turned away. This of course is the theory, but in practice there are a dozen paths in and out of the town, and all sorts of rogues and vagabonds come and go at will. Most of the buildings lie along the edge and to the west of Sutton Pool, and the Turk's Head stands in one of the maze of narrow alleys close to the harbour. Its landlord in those days was a Cornishman from across the Tamar, John Penryn; a black-haired, taciturn man, who made it his business to give good service, but never to inquire into the concerns of his guests. He knew nothing, saw nothing and heard nothing. As long as he was paid in full, that was all that mattered. Even if murder was committed beneath his roof, the Sheriff and county officers would receive no help from him.

Philip Underdown greeted him as an old friend, and I gathered that their association went back a long way, to the years when Philip and his brother were trading in and out of the town and had used the inn as their headquarters. There was a great deal of noise coming from the ale-room as we passed, but we were shown upstairs to a decent-sized chamber whose only door immediately faced the stairhead.

"You'll be comfortable enough here," the landlord said, and I fancied there was a hidden meaning to his words.

Philip Underdown nodded. "We'll take supper and breakfast in our room, if it's all the same to you. I don't wish to be seen more than necessary below stairs."

John Penryn inclined his head. "Moll can look after your meals. She's a good girl and doesn't complain at extra work." He paused with his hand on the latch. "Is there anyone you want me to watch out for?"

"Anyone who's a stranger. Particularly someone who's well-dressed, thin of face, dark-haired. Oh, and keep a weather eye cocked for Silas Bywater, though I doubt he'll be back in Plymouth before I leave tomorrow, unless he gets a lift from a passing carter. He's been to Buckfast for the St. Michael's fair and our paths unfortunately crossed."

The landlord curled his lip. "So that's where he was. I thought I hadn't seen him around for the past week. He's a born trouble-maker. He'll overstep the mark one of these days. I'll watch out for him, don't worry."

He disappeared and I heard him whistling as he went downstairs. I glanced about me and decided that the room was probably the best the inn afforded. There were two beds, I was happy to note, as I had no wish to share a mattress with my travelling companion, a large carved chest for clothes in one corner, and the rushes on the floor looked fairly clean with no sign of fleas hopping among them. The supper, too, when it came, was plentiful and wholesome, although mainly fish, it being a Friday. Philip grumbled, having had fish broth the previous evening; but, like me, he was too tired from the long day's ride to be very interested in what he was eating. And when the obliging girl called Moll had removed our dirty dishes and brought us our "all-night" of bread and ale, we both, of one accord, pulled off our boots, removed our outer clothing and fell into bed, sinking thankfully into the comfort of the feather-filled mattresses.

Nothing happened that night to disturb our rest, and the

morning sunlight was rimming the shutters before I was even conscious of closing my eyes. As I sat on the edge of the bed, yawning and stretching, I reflected contentedly that today would see me rid of my charge and free to return to Exeter to pick up my pack and resume my normal life, secure in the knowledge that I had successfully carried out the Duke's commission. Philip Underdown would be equally glad to see the back of me as he embarked for Brittany on board the *Falcon*.

John Penryn had promised to let us know the minute the *Falcon* was sighted as she made sail into the Cattewater beyond the Sutton Pool barrier. It was a fine day with the sea like a millpond, and there seemed to be no reason why the Master should not bring her in on time. But the morning passed, its brightness fading slowly into a more overcast afternoon, and still there was no sign of the ship. As four o'clock and supper-time approached once more, and as Philip Underdown and I grew yet more frustrated and edgy, we threw caution to the wind and went down to the harbour to ascertain for ourselves that the *Falcon* had indeed failed to arrive.

"Where the hell is she?" Philip demanded through clenched teeth. "The Duke assured me that the Master had his orders and would be here on Saturday with the tide."

I had no words of consolation to offer, and was busy reconciling myself to another evening and night in Philip Underdown's unwelcome company. I was quite as distressed by the turn of events as he was, and moved away abruptly before I showed my feelings too plainly. As I did so, I thought I saw a figure withdraw furtively into one of the alleys which ran between the houses lining the quay. But although I moved swiftly, when I peered into the noisome little street, its gutter thick with the rotting detritus of everyday life, I could see no one. At that time of day, with everyone at supper, all was as quiet as the grave.

CHAPTER

6

Neither of us slept well that night. To begin with, we were not tired. A day spent lazing in our room, with nothing to do but eat and doze, had left us wide awake and full of energy. Both of us were men used to hard work and constant activity, and such a state of idleness did not agree with our constitution. Over and above that, however, the *Falcon*'s failure to arrive on time was an irritating delay which we could well have done without, disliking as we did each other's company. But even that we might have endured with stoicism —for there are many reasons why a ship can be detained at sea—had it not been for my growing conviction that someone had been spying on us at the quayside.

My first inclination had been to blame an overheated imagination, but the more I thought about it, the more convinced I became that I had indeed seen a man loitering in the mouth of the alleyway.

"Then where did he go?" Philip demanded, with all the

truculence of one willing himself not to believe. "You say that when you looked, there was no one there."

"There were plenty of houses for him to step inside, on both sides of the street."

Philip Underdown snorted. "Hovels, all of them. A finical man like our friend from the Abbey would be disinclined to trust himself inside one of those." He laughed mockingly. "He might dirty his fine clothes."

But he was talking to convince himself. He knew as well as I did that if the man were a hired assassin, or a Woodville retainer, the fine clothes and delicate deportment were nothing more than a blind to mislead us. Such a man would not be put off by the consideration of muddying his dress.

These thoughts continued to haunt us throughout the evening, and proved the basis for a spasmodic, but acrimonious, discussion as we sat in our bedchamber, listening to the shouts and noisy laughter drifting up from the ale-room downstairs. And although these grated on our overstretched nerves, the comparative silence which followed the curfew bell was even worse. We finished the ale which the obliging Moll had brought us, and decided that it was time to sleep, neither of us anticipating much success.

Strangely enough, I was asleep almost before my head touched the pillow, but immediately I began to dream. It was the same dream I had had a month or so earlier, in the Hospital of St. Cross, in Winchester. I could again feel the wind on my face as I walked slowly forward beneath the interlacing trees, see the crescent moon above the clouds, feel the rough, stony path beneath my feet. And I was seized by the same all-pervading fear as I stumbled over the body . . .

I awoke once more in a state of sweat and panic, unsure for the moment of my surroundings. Then I heaved myself out of bed and crossed the room to open the shutters, which gave on to the yard at the back of the inn, taking in great gulps of salt sea air.

"What is it? What's the matter?"

I turned my head to make out Philip Underdown, his feet already out of bed, his dagger clasped in his right hand.

"Nothing," I said, feeling rather foolish. "A nightmare, that's all. I've suffered from them since childhood." My description was not strictly accurate, but I felt that to tell the truth, that my dreams were often like glimpses into the future, would be to lay myself open to even more of his contempt and scorn. As it was, he laughed derisively before lying down again.

"An uneasy conscience, perhaps," he suggested, not without malice.

"Perhaps." I was in no mood to argue. I leaned out to reclose the shutters, when I noticed, for the first time, the slip of crescent moon hanging above the chimney-pots of the town. The sense of foreboding gripped me yet again and I shivered. A breeze had sprung up, blowing in from the harbour, and as I reached for the second shutter, the noise of creaking wood sounded from somewhere below me. Glancing down, I saw that the shutters of the room immediately under ours were swinging wide on their hinges. Someone had prised them open in order to enter the inn.

"He's here!" I hissed at Philip. "He's in the house! There's no time to get help or try to trap him. Push one of the beds across the door."

He needed no second bidding; and even as we manœuvred his bed into position, there was a tell-tale groan from one of the stairs. It was a tread somewhere in the middle of the flight, and I had noticed its board was loose as we returned to our room yesterday afternoon. Moments later, the latch of the bedchamber door was quietly lifted and the door eased inwards, only to come up against the unyielding barrier of the bed. There was a second's pause before it was tried again; then, to the accompaniment of a faint, muffled curse, we heard footsteps retreating hurriedly down the stairs. I moved rapidly to the window and leaned out, hoping to catch a glimpse of the intruder, but he used the front door, as we discovered when we went in search of assistance, leaving it unbolted and standing open.

John Penryn, roused from sleep, was grimly apologetic, particularly when it was found that the downstairs shutter had been left unbarred, an oversight of which our enemy had taken full advantage. He must have been prowling round the inn, trying all the doors and windows; and I had not been awake yet again, we would have had a repetition of the incident at Buckfast, this time, perhaps, with fatal results.

After we had returned to our room, Philip to sleep in my bed and I in his, where he had replaced it across the doorway, I lay awake for a long time, thinking. Was tonight's intruder Silas Bywater, who had managed to return to Plymouth well ahead of the time expected by getting a ride from a passing carter? Alternatively, was he our assailant of the Abbey, and if so, who was he and what was he after? Was he an agent of the Woodvilles? In which case, he was more concerned with taking Philip's life than with the letter he was carrying. Or was he working for the Lancastrian dissidents, whose main aim must be to prevent Duke Francis of Brittany withdrawing his support from Henry Tudor? And to that end, King Edward's conciliatory missive had to be prevented from arriving.

There was, of course, a third possibility; that tonight's interloper had been neither Silas nor the gentleman of Buckfast, but a different assailant altogether, who, in his

turn, might be either a Woodville or a Lancastrian agent
. . . My head began to spin, and in spite of myself, I slept.

I awoke feeling neither refreshed nor rested, to find Philip
Underdown already up and dressed. The girl, Moll, was
tapping at the door, calling out that she had our shaving
water and breakfast outside, but could not get in. Quickly I
pulled on my boots and jacket and helped my companion
move the bed back to its normal place.

We shaved first, before the water cooled, but my black-
handled knife needed sharpening and I was left with almost as much stubble as I had started with. Philip cut
himself twice. We ate little, our appetites diminished by
worry and the uncertainties of another day. It was, moreover, Sunday, and the church bells were already summon-
ing people to Mass.

A sharp knock at the bedchamber door made us both
jump, such was the state of our nerves after the events of
the previous night. But it was only John Penryn.

"There's a man downstairs, asking for you by name,"
he said to Philip. "He said to give you this."

Philip took the silver disc which the landlord held out to
him and laid it down on his bed with a sigh of relief. I
could just make out from where I was sitting that it was
engraved with a coat-of-arms.

"Let him come up," he said. "He's a King's Messenger,
like me."

I stood up. "We'll come down, if you can find us a
corner of the ale-room where we shan't be overheard or
disturbed." I met Philip's furious gaze calmly. "There will
be safety in numbers. I don't suppose it's impossible to
steal one of those tokens, or to obtain it by other nefarious
means. If the landlord here and a couple of his men will
stay within call, I shall feel safer."

John Penryn gave me his backing, but in the event our caution was unnecessary. No sooner did Philip clap eyes on the other man than he hailed him by name.

"Simon Whitehead, what brings you to Plymouth?"

The newcomer, a short, sturdy man whose hair was so fair as to be nearly white, and whose eyelashes were almost invisible, motioned us both to sit opposite him at a table in the furthest corner of the ale-room from the door, where the landlord had placed him. Three mazers of ale stood ready for us, together with a dish of oatcakes. John Penryn and the two tapsters with him were waved away, and, satisfied that no danger threatened, they departed about the morning's business.

Simon Whitehead nodded at me. "Who's he?" he asked suspiciously.

"It's all right. He's the Duke of Gloucester's man," Philip answered, feeling, no doubt, that any other explanation would take too long. "You can talk in front of him. Where have you come from and how did you know I was here? You've obviously come to find me."

"I was on the King's business in Falmouth when news arrived that the Earl of Oxford has invested St. Michael's Mount. Three days ago, on the last day of September." Ignoring our exclamations of astonishment and horror, Simon Whitehead recruited his strength with a gulp of ale and continued: "Apparently he'd anchored in Mount's Bay, and then he and his followers—not above a hundred men in all, so I've been reliably informed—disguised themselves as pilgrims, with cloaks and broad-brimmed hats, waited for low tide and walked across the causeway as bold as you please. Said they were a group of palmers who had arrived by sea—true enough, I suppose—to make their offering at the shrine." Simon snorted in exasperation. "They were admitted without any questions being asked, and on reaching the upper court, threw off their cloaks, drew their swords—and that was that. They've expelled the monks and the garrison, and sent out raiding parties into the neighbouring villages for food. It goes without saying that they'll try to stir up insurrection, but I'll be surprised if they succeed. A few disaffected men perhaps, but no great numbers. Nevertheless, Sir Henry Bodrugan and the Sheriff, Sir John Arundel, have ordered all ships in the area to remain where they are for the time being, while messengers are despatched to London to inform the King of what has happened, and to receive his instructions. This, of course, includes the *Falcon*, which on Thursday was anchored in Falmouth roads. Is indeed still anchored there, awaiting developments. Fortunately, the Master knew me to be lodged in the town and had himself rowed ashore the following day in order to ask me to carry an urgent message, letting you know of the delay. Like me, he believes that King Edward will issue pressing orders for him to continue with his mission, but until these orders are actually received, the Master dare not disobey Sir Henry or Sir John."

"And in the meantime?" Philip Underdown's tones were clipped; his eyes held fear.

Simon Whitehead took a swig of ale and helped himself to another oatcake.

"You stay here." He shrugged. "The Turk's Head offers a comfortable enough billet. John Penryn will ask no questions. It will probably be only a matter of days."

"No." Philip slammed his empty mazer down on the table with a ferocity that made the other man jump. "I'll not stay here. There have been two attempts on my life the past two nights, and I'll not remain tamely waiting for a third."

The landlord, who was attending to our wants himself, overheard the last remark as he approached our table with a second jug of ale.

"There are always the cellars," he reminded Philip quietly. When the other man shook his head vehemently, he added: "No ghosts. Just the best ale and wine this side of the Tavy."

"And the duty not paid on any of it, I'll be bound," Simon Whitehead said, grinning.

John Penryn gave an answering grin, but made no comment, merely glancing in inquiry at Philip.

My companion was adamant. "No, I tell you! I'll not be mewed up down there." And he gave a slight, almost imperceptible shiver. "Why should I endure such discomfort?"

"Then we stay in our room," I said, "until such time as the *Falcon* drops anchor in the Cattewater. We can drag one bed across the door, as we did last night, and answer it to no one but Master Penryn or Moll. We should be sufficiently safe to guard against any intruder." But I have to admit that my heart sank as I made the suggestion. Five, possibly six, days of Philip Underdown's company in what would virtually be a prison was more than I could contemplate with any equanimity. And it would be all of that before the Sheriff's messengers could get to London and the King, even riding day and night, and bear his answer back again. And even when that was accomplished, the *Falcon* had still to sail up the coast to Plymouth.

It was almost with relief that I heard Philip say: "No! I'll not put up with it!" He looked at Simon Whitehead. "Are you returning to Falmouth?"

The other man glanced obliquely at the landlord, who circumspectly withdrew, leaving the jug of ale on the table. Simon refilled his mazer and answered: "I must. I have unfinished business there. Why? What is it you want me to do?"

"Get a message to the Master of the *Falcon*. Tell him I shall be in Plymouth again a week from today. Until then, I intend to lie up at Trenowth Manor, across the Tamar. Roger and I will leave tonight and cross by the ferry. After that, we ride northward under cover of darkness, arriving at Trenowth in time for breakfast."

I knit my brows. "And what tale do you tell the goodman of the house for wishing to remain a sennight under his roof? The weather is not yet severe enough to provide excuse."

"I shall tell Sir Peveril the truth. He and his lady are sworn supporters of the House of York. They'll not fail us."

Simon Whitehead chewed his lower lip. "I happen to know that Sir Peveril and Lady Trenowth have been in London since August, and mean to stay there until the winter."

"All the better. We can think of a story to satisfy the servants, and in any case they won't ask too many questions. This time of year, when the travelling minstrels and jugglers and acrobats are all settling into their winter quarters, life on the manor starts to get boring. They'll be glad of any distraction, and the women will be particularly pleased to see a fine young fellow like Roger here." Philip smiled suddenly, his teeth showing whitely against his tanned skin. "And of course, I shall be delighted to make any woman free of my company, whatever her age."

"You're familiar with Trenowth Manor?" I asked, not at all happy with the prospect thus sketched out for me. It seemed a foolish risk to take, when we might be reasonably safe at the Turk's Head. On the other hand, recalling my misgivings of a few minutes earlier, I realized that I was not so averse to the idea as I had at first thought.

"I know all this area as well as I know the environs of my native city. I told you, my brother and I worked out of Plymouth for many years." Philip folded his hands together on the table before him, regarding Simon Whitehead and myself with a challenging stare.

Simon Whitehead finished his ale. "It makes no difference to me where you wait. I'll certainly carry your message to the *Falcon's* Master, but after that, my part in this affair is finished. And now I must get some food, some rest and a change of horse before I start my ride back to Falmouth this afternoon. God be with you.''

He gave us both a brief nod before getting to his feet and going in search of John Penryn. My companion and I were left sitting at the table.

''What makes you think we won't be followed to Trenowth Manor?'' I asked. ''Our unknown gentleman has proved himself very persistent.''

''As I said, it'll be dark. There are a number of ways out of this town and John Penryn knows all of them. For a consideration, he and two of his men will go with us as far as the outskirts and make sure that we are not being followed. You can trust him.''

''And what of the horses? Two animals in the streets after curfew is bound to attract attention from the Watch.''

''Their hoofs will be muffled, and Penryn knows the hour in which every street is patrolled. The Watch can't be everywhere at once, or no felon would be able to make an honest living.'' He smiled thinly at his joke and emptied what remained in the jug into his mazer. ''You're too innocent, my friend. It's easy to see that you've had no dealings with criminals.''

I forbore to enlighten him, simply asking: ''And how do we get across the ferry?''

''We rouse the ferryman from sleep and dangle our purses in front of him. He'll take us across fast enough if there's money in it. So now, if we're to travel throughout the night, I suggest we get some rest. We'll need it if we're to make Trenowth by tomorrow morning.''

CHAPTER

7

We left the inn as soon as it was dark in the company of John Penryn. One of his men went ahead of us, making certain that the streets were clear of the Watch, while another walked some way behind, ensuring that we were not followed. That, at least, was the idea. For my own part, I was not convinced that a cellarman would be able to detect the presence of an expert in such matters who, of necessity, knew how to make himself inconspicuous, and who also had the cover of night to aid him. Philip Underdown seemed perfectly satisfied, however, so I held my peace.

The horses, after two days without exercise, were at first inclined to be frisky, even my staid rouncey, but they soon quietened down, quickly sensing, as animals do, the mood of people around them. By the time their hoofs had been muffled in torn-up strips of rags, they were growing docile, and they both behaved with almost perfect propriety as Philip and I led them through the maze of narrow alleys leading to the outskirts of the town. There was only one small incident as we passed a stable. The grey suddenly raised his head, nostrils flaring, and whinnied loudly. Philip cursed and tugged sharply on the reins, restoring silence, but not before the shutters of a house a little way ahead of us were thrown wide and a woman's head and shoulders were clearly visible, framed by the open window. She leaned forward and called: "Who's there?"

Philip hissed in my ear: "Don't answer. Just keep moving."

John Penryn nodded in agreement. "She won't make trouble," he whispered, "whoever she is. This is not a law-abiding part of the town."

Within ten minutes, we were free of Plymouth, emerging into the fields beyond and well clear of any of the gates and their custodians. Here the landlord and his men took leave of us, wishing us good luck, and returned the way they had come. Philip and I mounted our horses and rode west towards the ferryman's cottage at the edge of the Tamar. It was a still, dry night, the sky spangled with stars, and the crescent moon which I had observed in the small hours of this morning hanging low in the heavens. I felt again the prickle of fear along my spine and experienced once more the sense of foreboding.

All went as Philip had predicted at the ferry. The ferryman, roused from sleep, was at first angry and abusive, calling us all the insulting names he could lay his tongue to and throwing doubts on our parentage. This stream of abuse was halted abruptly by the sight of Philip's full purse and the promise of a shilling if he would take us and our horses across the river. As a shilling was worth several days' work to him, the man disappeared inside his cottage, emerging a few minutes later fully clothed.

By my reckoning it was already past midnight, for we must have ridden north-west of the town by some six or seven miles. And the ferryman's insistence that we go one at a time delayed us even further.

"One man, one horse," he announced in his gruff, surly tones. "It's for your own safety."

We agreed reluctantly. "I'll go first, with the cob," I said. "Waiting will only make me nervous."

Philip laughed. "You mean you don't trust me to wait for you if I go first. Don't worry. I've no intention of making a bolt for it. I've grown used to having you around."

I wasn't sure that I believed him, and in any case there was some truth in what I had said. I had crossed on ferries many times, but never before in the company of a horse; and although the animal was firmly secured, I was nevertheless extremely nervous. My relief at standing once more on dry ground was considerable, and I fancied that the cob felt the same way. He nuzzled my face affectionately as we watched the ferry depart on its return journey for Philip and his mount. I glanced about me.

As far as I could tell in the darkness, we were standing on a spit of sand running some few yards out into the water. Behind us lay a little beach, and beyond that the land rose gently to a belt of trees, the edge of the forests covering this part of Cornwall. The river, which narrowed at this particular point, but which was still too wide for the horses to swim across, rippled between the banks on an outgoing tide. The opposite shore rose steeply to a cliff-top where stunted trees and bushes clung precariously in the teeth of the gales which must surely batter that coast each winter. Even on such a calm night, they swayed slightly to the rhythm of a freshening breeze, dipping and curtseying; flat, black shapes silhouetted against the faintly luminous skyline.

I stiffened suddenly and my fingers tightened on the cob's reins. Surely there had been someone up there, on the clifftop, standing perfectly still, looking down on the scene below him. I screwed up my eyes, straining to see through the enveloping darkness. But there was nothing there except the bushes and wind-bitten trees. I stared long and hard, searching for a telltale movement, until forced to give up by the irritation of trying not to blink. I upbraided myself that I was getting jumpy, beginning to imagine danger where none existed. Yet I continued to peer at the distant cliff-top, not entirely convinced that I had been mistaken.

The raft made its slow return across the river, the ferryman steering skilfully to allow for the swiftly running current and eventually depositing Philip Underdown and his grey safely on Cornish soil. The man held out his hand for his money, and when this had been paid, we mounted and turned the horses' heads inshore.

Philip looked over his shoulder. "Remember! If anyone asks, you haven't seen us. No one has crossed during the night. Is that understood?"

The ferryman muttered something which might have been assent and which seemed to satisfy my companion. For my own part, I was doubtful, conjecturing that if he were offered enough to betray us, the man would do so without any qualm of conscience. I said as much to Philip as we rode inland from the strand towards the belt of trees.

He shrugged. "It's a chance we have to take. He may be afraid of retribution should we return this way. It was worth giving him a warning."

I wondered if I should tell him that I thought our crossing had already been overlooked, but I was so unsure of whether or not I had really seen anything at all that I decided to remain silent. Just in case my eyes had not deceived me, I would be extra vigilant.

Before we reached the edge of the woods, we turned off along a track which skirted the river for a while, then

turned inland where the trees receded. I was deeply relieved, having been afraid that Philip's intention was to use
the forest paths which, however great their concealment,
were likely to be infested with outlaws and robbers. I had
contemplated remonstration, expecting to be informed that
he knew this countryside like the back of his hand and that
he had no fear of a few cut-throats and footpads; but, as it
turned out, I was thankful I had not laid myself open to
ridicule. As it was, I was uneasy enough and frequently
touched my "Plymouth cloak," where it lay across my saddle-bow, for reassurance.

We made a steady pace, avoiding wherever possible any
hamlets or straggling clusters of cottages in our path. The
river flowed seawards on our right, while to our left,
the dimly seen fields and ploughed strips belonging to the
smaller settlements were lapped about, and often en-
croached upon, by the billowing forest. This was a land of
abundant vegetation; in daylight, opulent, intrusive upon
the eye like neighbouring Devon. We stopped twice to rest
and refresh ourselves with the food provided for the journey by John Penryn; once under a brake of gorse, the second time in a deserted stone hut, long abandoned by some
goat-herd or shepherd. Our conversation, when we talked
at all, was desultory, speculating on the King's reaction to
events on St. Michael's Mount.

"Couldn't you have waited and found another ship to
carry you to Brittany?" I asked at one point.

Philip Underdown was scathing. "And fallen into the
hands of Lancastrians posing as good, honest fishermen or
merchants? No! I'll wait for the *Falcon*."

I caught his response with only half an ear, listening as I
was for the quiet clop of a horse's hoofs, carrying our
pursuer. But all I could hear was the soughing of the breeze
through the distant trees and the soothing murmur of running water.

We were, according to Philip, about a mile from Trenowth when we stopped for the third and final time, dismounting and leading our horses down to the river's edge to wash our faces in the ice-cold water. The two animals drank thirstily while we attempted to rid ourselves of the night's growth of beard and brushed down our crumpled and travel-stained clothing. It was already light with the promise of a beautiful day. The early morning mist lifted and swam about us like spun silk; drifting, billowing folds, beaded here and there with trembling pendants of gold. Then the sun rose, gilding the clouds, and the mist dispersed, leaving the damp earth gently steaming.

Philip yawned and stretched. "I shan't be sorry to get breakfast inside me," he said. "Let's hope it's hot and there's plenty of it."

I agreed. My stomach was rumbling with hunger in spite of the cold meat pasties we had consumed less than two hours previously. I led the cob to the top of the bank and stood staring back the way we had come, the track barred with stripes of sunshine and dappled shadow. I remained perfectly still and quiet, but again there was nothing to hear except the singing of the birds, nothing to see except their fluttering in and out of the trees.

Trenowth Manor stood high above the Tamar, on a wide plateau of land overlooking the river's thickly wooded banks. The home of Sir Peveril and Lady Trenowth was built around an inner quadrangle, its grey granite walls presenting narrow apertures and a frowning aspect to the outside world, with more gracious doors and windows opening upon the courtyard. As we rode up the steep slope to the gatehouse, we could see that the servants were already abroad, the gate standing wide and two men unloading sacks of flour which had been brought up by cart from the corn mill. Philip approached them.

"Is your master at home? Tell him his old friend Philip Underdown wishes to see him."

I could almost have believed myself that he was a friend of Sir Peveril, he spoke with such confidence, and it was not at all surprising that both men immediately stopped what they were doing and came to attend to his wants.

"Master's from home, sir," one of them said, pulling at his forelock.

"Mistress, too," the other man put in, thus confirming what Simon Whitehead had told us.

"Up London," the first one went on, obviously irritated by his companion's intervention and frowning him down. "King's business," he added importantly. "Said 'e won' be back for a long time."

I had been half afraid that we should find they spoke nothing but Cornish, but the broad, flat vowels were reminiscent of speech across the Tamar, in Devon, and English was plainly their native language.

"Ah!" Philip did his best to look nonplussed, as though sizing up an unexpected situation. "This is awkward. My man and I have been on the road for several days and were looking to rest for a while at Trenowth, but in the circumstances . . ." He completed the sentence with an eloquent little shrug and lapsed into silence.

"Wait there, sir," the second obliging fellow instructed. "I'll fetch Alwyn Steward to you directly."

He hurried off, returning after some four or five minutes with the steward, a tall, thin, slightly balding man who stooped, as though permanently bent to listen to other people's inquiries. His watery blue eyes passed over me to rest on Philip, thereby demonstrating how right my companion had been to designate us man and master.

Philip repeated his story with even more confidence,

now that he was absolutely certain there was no chance of Sir Peveril returning home to gainsay it. The steward frowned a little in an effort to recall his name. "You say, sir, you're a friend of my master's?"

"In London. He and Lady Trenowth have often urged me to stay with them if ever I found myself in this part of Cornwall." He dismounted and drew Alwyn to one side. I saw the flash of silver as, presumably, he showed the man his own token of credence, such as the one Simon Whitehead had been carrying, and heard him mutter the words "King's business."

The steward looked impressed and, I guessed, would be even more so later, when Philip swore him to secrecy.

"You must come in, sir, and rest here as many days as you wish. My master and mistress would never forgive me if I failed to offer hospitality to their friends. Sir Peveril will be sorry to have missed you."

He led the way beneath the arch of the gatehouse, the horses' hoofs echoing hollowly on the cobbles, and requested us to wait while he went in search of the housekeeper. During his absence, I took stock of my surroundings.

Two sides of the quadrangle, the one facing us and to our left, were the family living quarters, demonstrated by the fact that the buildings were two-storeyed. There was ample room for a large brood of children, but I learned later from the housekeeper that Sir Peveril and Lady Trenowth had not been so blessed. The laundry and dairy lay to one side of the gateway, the bakehouse to the other, the doors standing open to reveal the inmates hard at work. There seemed to be no slacking because the master and mistress were from home, a fact which argued for contented and well-treated servants. The savoury and mouthwatering smells drifting out of an open doorway in the right-hand corner of the courtyard told me that the kitchens could not be far away. And they were probably, as is usual, flanked by the buttery. The low building to our right must therefore be the servants' quarters.

The steward came fussing back, with apologies for keeping us waiting. In the absence of Sir Peveril and Lady Trenowth he was assuming full responsibility for the day-to-day running of the manor.

"I have spoken to Janet Overy," he said, "and she will prepare beds for you. You will have the guest chamber next to Sir Peveril's, Master Underdown, and a truckle-bed will be set up for your man. Unless, of course, you wish him to sleep in the servants' quarters or the kitchen."

I sent Philip a warning glance which dared him to choose either of the latter. I could see that he was tempted, and had he not been so shaken by recent events, he might have done so out of a perverted sense of humour. As it was, he said quietly: "My man will sleep with me."

Alwyn nodded. "So Mistress Overy and I expected." A door opened from the servants' quarters and he turned his head. "Ah! Here is Mistress Overy now. For the present, I will leave you in her capable hands. When you are settled just send for me. I must go. With the master and Lady Trenowth away, there is much to see to."

He bustled importantly about his business, hurrying across the courtyard, the hem of his gown clinging around his thin ankles, and disappeared through the main door at the top of a shallow flight of steps which spanned the undercroft. Philip and I shifted our gaze to the house-keeper.

She was a handsome woman, not in the first flush of youth, and I guessed her to be somewhere in her mid-thirties. She wore a black woollen dress, with an apron and gorget of fine white linen. Her head was covered by a black silk hood, but a tendril of hair escaping from beneath it indicated that she had the fair Saxon colouring suggested by her blue eyes and pale skin. A large bunch of keys attached to her belt demonstrated her importance in the household. She had a most pleasant smile, but there was a steely glint in her eyes and a determined set to her mouth which boded ill for any underling who did not know his or her place. She looked a capable woman and one whom I should not care to cross.

She was within a few paces of us when she suddenly paused, screwing up her eyes as though to bring us better into focus. The early morning sun was full in our faces, and she moved a little to one side where the shadow of the gatehouse wall afforded her clearer visibility.

"You!" she said, staring at Philip.

He returned her scrutiny with interest, attracted, as by his own admission he always was, by any good-looking woman. "Do we know each other?" he asked, smiling.

The housekeeper laughed, a low, musical sound, full-throated and with genuine amusement.

"Oh, not to speak to. But I've seen you around these parts before, four, maybe five years ago . . . Surely, I'm not mistaken." She tilted her head to one side, regarding him with patent admiration. "I'm certain I couldn't mix up a handsome, well-built man like you with anyone else, now could I?"

It was his turn to laugh. I watched him swell with vanity, puffed up with pride that she remembered him.

"You're right. My brother—God assoil him!—was with me then. We were traders, buying and selling. But I don't recall you at Trenowth in those days."

"I wasn't. I lived across the river, on the Devon side of the water. A widow woman then, as indeed I am still, but today I have this snug billet. However," she added, recollecting her duties, "we can talk later, when you've washed and eaten. Please follow me, Master Underdown, and your man, if he will. I'll show you to your quarters."

CHAPTER
8

 We were housed in a corner room above the great chamber, its only door opening into a narrow corridor which led from the head of the main staircase, past the entrance to a second guest-chamber which was at present empty.

"We have few guests when the master's away," Janet Overy said, ushering us both inside. "Alwyn Steward and I thought this room the pleasanter of the two because of the window." She indicated the open shutter which allowed the early October sunshine to filter through panes of leaded glass, an unusual luxury in an upstairs chamber and doubly so in a bedroom. "Sir Peveril had this done last year, when he had the honour of entertaining the Sheriff for two or three nights. A truckle-bed will be brought up by the men while you are having your breakfast. Yours, Master Underdown, will be laid in the great hall." She nodded at me. "You, fellow, can come to the kitchen."

Philip shook his head. "If it's all the same to you, Mistress, I'll eat in the kitchen with Roger here. I've no mind to sit in solitary state. That goes for all my meals through-out our stay, which, as far as I can calculate, will probably be for a sennight. The steward knows the ins and outs of it. Which reminds me, I want a further word with him after breakfast." He glanced around at the bed, the cedarwood chest in one corner, the bedside table on which stood a pewter jug and plate, ready for the "all-night." "Where's the garderobe?"

"At the end of the corridor, near the top of the stairs. One of the girls will bring you water to wash, and there's a pump in the courtyard for your man if he wants it." Janet Overy looked at me as if seeing me clearly for the first time, and not just as a servant of Philip Underdown. I thought she seemed faintly surprised, as though I was not what she would have expected; but the expression was so fleeting that I decided I might have been mistaken. She added: "Come down to the kitchens for your breakfast when you're ready. It will be waiting for you." She went out and closed the door.

Philip threw himself down on the bed, chuckling. "Wasn't this a good idea of mine? A soft lodging for as long as we want it. I'm sorry to delegate to you the role of servant, but it would have looked strange if I had been travelling without one."

His tone was cheerful, and I guessed that he was not at all sorry. It gave him a feeling of power and restored some of the pride my unwelcome presence had eroded. I said nothing, but crossed to the window, opened it and looked out. Because the aspect was south-facing, and the Cornish climate generally mild, someone, at some time, had planted a vine against the wall; a vine which had grown strongly and sturdily over the years so that now its leaves and tendrils embraced three sides of the window aperture. This had led to a single shutter being fitted, instead of the more usual two, which, when open, lay back flat against the wall on the left-hand side. The prospect immediately in view was of an open stretch of grassland, falling away sharply to the wooded banks of the river and the broad, well-worn track up which we had ridden a little earlier that morning.

I breathed deeply. The air was sweet and mild, and I could smell the scents of the river as it ran, unseen, somewhere below us, flowing from distant uplands to the open sea. Then, at Philip's impatient instigation, I drew my head back into the room and set about unpacking my bundle. Not that there was much to unpack, and it was soon done, my spare shirt flung atop the chest and my black-handled knife, which served me so faithfully for so many purposes, tucked into my belt alongside my pouch with its small store of money. I took hold of my cudgel.

"For the love of Mary, why carry that with you?" Philip demanded irritably. "Leave it here."

I shook my head obstinately. "We'll take a look around after we've eaten. I'll feel safer if I have it with me."

Philip shrugged. "Please yourself. I need the garderobe, so let's be going. I'll use it on the way down."

We both used it and, feeling more comfortable, proceeded downstairs, through the great chamber and across the courtyard to the kitchen. This seemed full of people, it obviously being the hour at which some of the household broke their night's fast after attending to the first chores of the day. A kitchenmaid was stirring a large pot over the fire, while another was unpacking the loaves of hot bread which she had just fetched in a basket from the bakehouse. The two men who had been unloading sacks of flour when we arrived were seated on a bench by one wall, bowls and spoons in hand, waiting expectantly. Alwyn the steward was overseeing the laying of his place at the centre table, fussily instructing a third small kitchenmaid in her duties, while Janet Overy calmly moved from one spot to another, making sure that everything was as it should be. But none of these held our attention as did the woman already seated at the end of the table, a little aloof from the rest of her companions, eating an apple.

"Jesus!" Philip breathed in my ear. "What a marvel!"

And indeed, his enthusiasm was justified. I have known some beautiful women in my time, but very few who could match the red-haired, green-eyed voluptuousness of Isobel Warden—for so she was introduced to us.

"The wife," Janet Overy said, with, I thought, a warning edge to her voice, "of our bailiff, Edgar."

But if she were trying to put us on our guard, Philip ignored her. Isobel Warden presented too great a challenge to be withstood. He went to sit beside her, swinging his legs agilely over the bench, the veins on his thick neck knotted like cords. The woman—for, young as she undoubtedly was, it was impossible to think of her as a girl—glanced sideways at him. Philip slid an arm around her waist and squeezed it. Isobel raised no objection.

She was an extraordinarily bold woman, and I don't think I have ever met another quite like her. The other members of the household were obviously used to her, but disapproving none the less. Janet Overy frowned and Alwyn looked down his nose as though he had just got a whiff of the sewers. The three kitchenmaids started to giggle in the affected way which betokens embarrassment rather than genuine amusement, while the two men muttered angrily to each other, their sympathies plainly with the absent husband.

The housekeeper took a bowl of thick gruel from one of the girls and placed it in front of Philip. "Eat this, Master Underdown," she said, "and leave Isobel alone. She has a man of her own who is very jealous of her." She smiled in propitiation. "There are plenty of single women, or widows like me, without men having to steal from one another."

Philip laughed, and I frowned at him as I took my seat by his side. He returned my look mockingly and, in defiance of us all, once again put his arm around Isobel Warden's shapely waist. "You don't mind, sweetheart, do you?" he asked, adding for the benefit of the rest of us: "She likes me."

While he was speaking, a shadow had fallen across the open doorway and now there was a great bellow of rage from the man who stood there; a young man with curling black hair and a massive frame, his hands bunched into two admirable fists.

"Leave my woman alone!" he shouted and was across the room in two strides to lift Philip bodily off the bench, twist him round and floor him with a crashing blow to his jaw. It all happened so quickly that no one, including myself, had time to intervene.

I was, however, swift enough to get astride my companion's recumbent form before the infuriated young Hercules could launch another attack, his clawed hands suggesting that he was about to follow up by trying to throttle Philip. Instead, they closed around my upper arms.

"Get out of my way!" the bailiff thundered.

"You'll have to make me," I answered.

"Stop this unseemly brawling immediately!" Alwyn thrust his steward's white staff between us. "Edgar, this man is a friend of Sir Peveril, and you will treat him as you would if the master were present. Heed what I say or I shall be forced to dismiss you. As for you, sir," he went on, addressing Philip, who was scrambling undignifiedly to his feet, "please have the kindness to treat our womenfolk with the courtesy they deserve. And you, woman," he continued, turning on Isobel, "try to recollect that you are now married, and keep you favours for your husband."

I should not have believed that such an ineffectual-looking man could have wielded such authority, had I not witnessed it with my own eyes. Edgar still looked sullen enough to wish for vengeance, but he sat down at the table without argument, contenting himself with giving his wife a glance which boded her no good. Philip, too, resumed his place, although his cut and swelling jaw was going to mar his enjoyment of the food for several meals to come. Only the cause of all the trouble appeared unmoved by the steward's admonitions, and went on placidly eating her apple.

Mistress Overy would have attended to Philip's hurt at once, but he waved her away, determined to make light of his injuries. And indeed, it was his pride which had been wounded far more than his body, as I could tell by his furious expression. Well, he had brought it on himself. I was in no mood to waste my sympathy on him.

The meal was eaten in uncomfortable silence, with only the housekeeper and myself making any attempt at conversation. When it was over, Philip announced that he was going to his room to rest. I followed him across the courtyard, through the great chamber and up to the narrow, twisting staircase to the rooms above. He turned on me irritably.

"Do we have to go everywhere together?"

I returned his look coolly. "I think it wisest, don't you?"

He hesitated, then shrugged. "Perhaps, in the circumstances." He moved towards the bed. "I'm tired after riding all night. I intend to sleep." He laughed nastily. "What a pity they haven't yet brought up the truckle-bed." He broke off abruptly, his eyes fixed on the open window. "There's someone there, among the trees." He turned, painfully gripping my arm. "I saw him."

I tried to be reassuring, although my heart was beating

unpleasantly fast. "It's probably one of Sir Peveril's men. You heard what Mistress Overy was saying at breakfast. The corn mill and the saw-pit and the forge are all out of sight of the house, on the edge of the estate. There are bound to be people coming and going all day."

Philip shook his head. "No. This man saw me looking and immediately dodged behind one of the trees. I think you ought to go and investigate. I'll stay here. You won't come to any harm on your own."

"Very well," I agreed reluctantly. "But lock the door while I'm gone."

I took my cudgel and went downstairs again. As I crossed the courtyard to the gatehouse arch, I heard my rouncey whinny softly from the stables, next to the servants' quarters. It was amazing how, in just a few days I had grown to know his sound and smell and touch. I should hate parting with him when it came time to return him to the Bishop's stable at Exeter. I was tempted to go and see him, to make sure that he had been properly fed and watered after his long night ride; but I knew I must not allow our intruder, if there was one, time to get away, and in any case I could trust Sir Peveril's groom to know his job.

One of the laundrywomen emerged from the laundry, carrying a basket of washing under one arm. She gave me good-day and followed me under the arch into the meadow, where she began spreading out the wet clothes on the grass to dry. I went on my way towards the belt of trees, plunging down the track which led to the river's edge, slowing my pace and peering cautiously from one side to the other. The bright sunlight paled and dimmed, struggling to penetrate the interlaced branches overhead. The leaves were already turning, and occasionally the breeze would shake some loose, floating them to earth like delicate flakes of beaten copper.

Gripping my cudgel more firmly, I left the track and began to explore among the undergrowth, where last year's leafmould still clung about the trunks and roots of stunted young trees, unable to force their way upwards into the light. It was very quiet and from time to time I paused, hearing nothing but the thudding of my heart. Once, from the path now hidden from my view, I heard the rumble of a cart and the shout of the carter to his assistant to "mind that those logs at the back are tied securely!"; firewood for the coming winter was being carried from the saw-pit up to the house.

I had no sense of being watched, only a feeling of being completely alone. In spite of what I myself thought I had seen at the ferry crossing, I was seized by the growing conviction that Philip had in fact seen nothing, and that he had deliberately got me out of the way while he went in search of Isobel Warden. It would now be an object with him to revenge himself upon the bailiff, and in what better way could he do that than by seducing his wife? Common sense told me that even Philip Underdown would not be so foolish, yet I found myself crashing through the trees and running up the track to the gatehouse as though the Green Man himself were at my heels. I ran across the courtyard and the great chamber, took the stairs three at a time and burst into our room . . .

Philip was sprawled, sound asleep and snoring, on the bed.

Feeling extremely foolish and more than a little ashamed of my suspicions, I gently closed the door on his recumbent form and wondered what to do next. It seemed pointless to return immediately to the woods to carry on my search. If there had indeed been anyone there, he would have withdrawn long ago, disturbed by my noisy exit. I realized that although it was probably less than an hour since breakfast, my walk had made me hungry again, so I made way to the kitchen in the hope of finding something more to eat.

The courtyard was bustling now, with people coming and going about their daily work, but the kitchen was temporarily deserted by everyone except Janet Overy, who was standing at a long table at the far end of the room, checking the day's produce which had evidently been brought by one of the men from the walled garden at the back of the house. She turned when she heard me come in and smiled.

"Are you hungry?" she asked, wiping her hands on a cloth and advancing towards me.

"How did you guess?" I asked sheepishly. "I must have eaten enough for two at breakfast."

She laughed. "Get away with you! A great lad like you needs constant sustenance. I know. I was married to one myself." She bade me sit down, producing bread and cheese and a plate of almond milk doucettes, which she told me she had baked freshly that morning. Then she filled a mazer with ale, drawn from a cask in the corner, and sat down to keep me company at the table. She looked hot and flushed from the warmth of the kitchen, and I guessed she was glad to rest for a moment. "You remind me somewhat of my husband," she added.

"Have you been widowed long?" I asked through a mouthful of bread and cheese.

Sorrow veiled her face. "Eight or nine years. Maybe more. Time passes so swiftly, it's not always easy to keep track of its flight. Hugh was a fisherman—he owned his own boat. He and two of his men were drowned at sea a week before our son was born."

I paused in the act of raising the mazer to my lips and stretched out a hand to lay it over one of hers. "I'm sorry. But the boy must be a great comfort to you."

I knew I had said the wrong thing by the look on her face. It was like the shadow of death as it fans from chin to brow, flattening the features and emptying them of all animation.

"I lost him," she said, "when he was five years old. One of the loveliest children you ever saw, as fair-haired and blue-eyed as you are. But that's enough of me and my affairs." She spoke with a fierce, determined cheerfulness, daring me to pursue the subject. "Tell me about yourself. What are you doing with Master Underdown? You're too young to have been with him in the old days."

I had foreseen the question and had been wondering just how much of the truth I could impart if she asked it. There was no doubt that Alwyn the steward had been the recipient, to some extent, of Philip's confidence, and I was unsure how far he could be trusted to say nothing at all to Mistress Overy, his nearest in rank and importance among the servants. Besides, if Philip and I had been followed from Plymouth, extra vigilance from additional pairs of eyes could do us no harm and might even forestall any danger. Moreover, the responsibility for my companion's safety was beginning to weigh heavily on my shoulders. The two days which the Duke had imposed on me had stretched now to five, with more yet to come. I needed to share my burden with someone, and Mistress Overy, although of course younger, reminded me very much of my mother. She had the same air of serenity, of having all life's answers, that my mother had possessed; the ability to lure secrets out of you, even when you have determined to say nothing. I knew I should probably confide in no one, but the desire to talk was overwhelming.

I looked over my shoulder to make sure that we were still alone, gave a nervous glance at the open door and window, lowered my voice almost to a whisper and plunged into my story.

CHAPTER
9

 When I had finished speaking, Janet Overy rose and refilled my mazer, then resumed her place at the table, folding her hands in front of her.

"A remarkable story," she said, "with another behind it that you haven't told me, or why would so important a personage as the King's own brother have picked on you for such a mission? Rest assured, I shall certainly keep my eyes open for any strangers about the manor. As for Silas Bywater, I think I know the man you mean. I recollect seeing him once in Master Underdown's company when I went to Plymouth for stores. My son was with me at the time." She changed the subject abruptly, balking at memories which were too painful to bear.

"You'll keep what I've told you to yourself," I urged. "Although I think Alwyn may know something."

She smiled. "I don't gossip with kitchen-maids . . . What was that?" She rose suddenly from the table, one finger held up in warning. On silent feet, she crossed to the door and looked outside, while I watched her anxiously.

After a moment or two she turned round with a shake of her head. "There's no one there. I'm hearing things. In any case," she added optimistically, "I don't think anyone could have overheard us. We've been keeping our voices low."

Relieved, but not quite convinced, I went outside to see for myself. The courtyard was still busy—the logs which I had earlier heard being carted up the track were now safely unloaded and stowed beneath the undercroft—but there was no one near the kitchen. I went back inside to finish the last of the doucettes. As I did so, I remembered something and opened the pouch attached to my belt, pulling out the limp, withering stem of knotgrass.

"This is what Silas Bywater asked me to give Master Underdown. Does it mean anything to you?"

The housekeeper picked it up and stared curiously at it before shaking her head. "It's just knotgrass, as you told me. It's a common enough weed."

"My mother once told me that it was poisonous."

Mistress Overy looked doubtful. "I've never heard that said of it. But I don't know everything," she admitted cheerfully, "and your mother could have been right." She put her head on one side, considering me. "I thought you said Philip Underdown threw it away after you'd shown it to him. If that was the case, how do you still come to have it?"

"I picked it up and put it in my pouch when he wasn't looking. Don't ask me why. I suppose I was just curious about it and the effect it had on him. I could see that it meant something, even though he strenuously denied it. I'd forgotten about it until just now. Here, I'll get rid of it."

I carried the grass to the door and tossed it outside. A small breeze caught it, whirling it up into the air, then dropping it in the dust of the courtyard.

"I'm keeping you from your work," I said. "Thank you for the food and for listening to me. I'll go now."

"Get some rest," she advised me, "like your so-called master. James and Luke should have taken the truckle-bed up to your room by now. I'll send one of them to wake you if I see or hear anything suspicious. After being up all night, you must be tired."

I acknowledged the fact and thanked her yet again. I was glad I had told her the truth. Janet Overy was a capable woman, and I trusted her ability to do as she had promised. Furthermore, there was a good stout lock on the bed-chamber door and a key to go with it. Neither Philip nor I could be surprised by anyone, provided I shut the window, for the vine worried me a little. When I reached the room, I found that the truckle-bed had indeed been set up against one wall, but its arrival appeared not to have disturbed my companion, who was still snoring lustily.

I laid down my cudgel, kicked off my boots and, without even stopping to remove my jacket, dropped on to the narrow mattress and was soon as soundly asleep as Philip. And, for all I know, as loudly snoring.

The sun was high in the sky when I awoke, and pouring in through the leaded panes of the window. Philip was sitting up on his bed, watching me closely.

"Ah," he said, swinging his feet to the ground, "you're awake at last, are you? I've been thinking."

I was barely attending to his words, caught as I was by the sudden realization that I had exchanged one prison for another; the Turk's Head for Trenowth Manor, and that there was still a week of Philip Underdown's company to be endured before I was finally relieved of my charge. More, perhaps, if the situation on St. Michael's Mount convinced King Edward that the *Falcon* must remain where she was. I thought longingly of my own company, the open road and freedom from care as I peddled my wares from one village to another. If only I had decided against visiting Exeter last Thursday morning, I should not now be wet-nursing a man I found it increasingly difficult to like.

I became aware that Philip was thrusting something at me. "So here," he said, "you take it."

"W-what?" I stuttered, trying to gather my thoughts together.

He almost spat in exasperation. "You haven't listened to a word I've been saying. I want you to keep the King's letter until it's time for me to embark at Plymouth next week—if all goes well, that is." His reservations uncomfortably echoed my own. "Put it somewhere safe."

"Why?" I demanded, making no move to accept the letter from him.

"Because, as I have just explained, while your wits were plainly wool-gathering, if—which St. Michael and all his angels forfend!—anything should happen to me, it could be the first thing my attacker would look for about my person. No one," he sneered, "would think of you carrying it. Put it in your pouch and guard it with your life." The look he gave me implied that this was not a very valuable commodity.

I could see the force of his argument and was faintly surprised that he should show so much concern and foresight for his mission. Until now, he had behaved, in spite of all that had happened to him, as if he were immune to danger. But at last he was beginning to act like a sensible man, conscious of his responsibilities. It was not therefore for me to discourage him. I took the letter, sealed with the royal seal, and put it into my pouch as he requested. I felt weighed down even further, as though my burden had increased tenfold.

It suddenly occurred to me that he had not asked about

the stranger he swore he had seen that morning from the window. An odd omission for someone who had displayed so much anxiety at the time. And now I came to think of it, it was also strange that he had not stayed awake long enough for my report, but had fallen asleep on the bed. My earlier uneasiness returned. What had he been up to in my absence?

"Isobel Warden," I began abruptly, then hesitated.

"What about her?"

"It would be foolish to antagonize the husband. We have other enemies to think about. To make another, deliberately, of the bailiff would be courting unnecessary trouble."

The curl of his lip became more pronounced. "Do you think I'm a fool? I can work that out for myself."

"I think you're rash and can be hasty when provoked. Although in this case, it was you who offered the provocation."

He turned his head so that the light from the window fell on his bruised lip and swollen jaw. "You don't call this provocation?"

"No. Retaliation. You knew the lady was married before you touched her."

Philip laughed and sat down again on the edge of his bed. "Holy Mother preserve us! What a prudish, pious young man you are, Roger Chapman! And if you think Isobel Warden is a lady, let me tell you you're mistaken. That woman is a harlot if ever I saw one. Before their marriage is much older, her husband will have more to get angry about than one arm around her waist and a gentle squeeze."

"That's as may be," I answered, swallowing my resentment at his reading of my character. "But that's between him and her. Our priority is to make as little stir here as possible. If Edgar Warden starts complaining about you in the local ale-house, your whereabouts will soon be common property. We need to lie low. And since you have still failed to ask, I found no one in the woods this morning."

"What?" He stared at me for a moment, obviously puzzled. Then he recollected. "Oh . . . Yes." He seemed disconcerted, unsure how to reason away his forgetfulness. "I came to the conclusion, after you had gone, that I had been mistaken. What I saw was no more than a shadow of some branches moving in the breeze." It was a lame explanation and he knew it. Before I could cavil, he got swiftly to his feet. "Judging by the sun, it must be nearly noon. Dinner will be eaten and cleared away if we don't hurry."

I let the matter drop, but resolved to keep an even closer eye on Philip and not let myself be duped again. But the suspicion that he had used my absence for some purpose of his own was stronger than ever.

The rest of the day passed as I feared much of the week before us must pass, eating and dozing and eating again. The life of the manor went on around us, but we had no active part to play. Philip attributed the servants' lack of curiosity about us to whatever explanation of our presence the steward had seen fit to give them.

"For you must know," he said, "that I felt it necessary to tell Alwyn at least some of the truth."

"I guessed as much." I forbore to mention that I had imparted the whole story, including some bits of it which I was sure he would rather not have had told, to Janet Overy. If the lady kept her counsel, as I felt certain she would, I saw no need to excite his anger. The only thing which worried me was Janet's fear that we might have been overheard, in spite of her later conviction that we could not have been.

Neither of us strayed from the courtyard, spending the

afternoon with our backs propped against a wall of the house, basking in the frail warmth of the October sun and waiting until it should be four o'clock and supper-time. I guessed Philip was beginning to realize, as I had already done, that Trenowth Manor offered little more in the way of diversion than the Turk's Head, and hoped that he would become reconciled to the fact. Otherwise, he was likely to try and make his own amusement, an attempt which would inevitably, in my view, involve Isobel Warden.

We attended Vespers in the manor chapel, which, on this Eve of St. Faith, was conducted by the parish priest in the absence of the Trenowth chaplain, who had accompanied his master and mistress to London. He came fussing across the courtyard, hot and flustered and with apologies for being late, just as we were sitting down to supper. His rheumy old eyes brightened at the sight of the laden table, and there was no possibility of his refusing to stay and share it after the service. When we were all once more assembled in the kitchen and seated round the table, the first rumblings of hunger appeased by boiled chicken, bacon and peas, he allowed his attention to wander, settling it on Philip and myself.

"Alwyn has been telling me that you are a friend of Sir Peveril," he said to Philip, "and that you are travelling in this part of the country." He raised his shaggy eyebrows, plainly inviting further confidences, but Philip merely grunted and continued eating. The priest went on unctuously: "Sir Peveril is a good man. A great benefactor of the church."

"A very fine fellow," Philip agreed and helped himself to a second portion of chicken.

"As for you, sir," the priest, whom the others addressed as Father Anselm, persevered, "may I say how pleasant it is to find a gentleman who does not object to taking his meals with the lowlier members of the household and a humble parish priest, such as myself."

"I don't like eating alone," Philip answered brusquely, cramming his mouth with food and so preventing himself from speaking further.

Father Anselm smiled thinly, accepting that he was being bested in a game at which he normally excelled; extracting information from other people. "Nevertheless, I regard it as praiseworthy that you do not hold aloof from your fellow men, unlike the other stranger in our midst who arrived at the ale-house in the village this morning. Not only did he not come to church for Vespers, but Thomas Aylward, the landlord, tells me that he has not deigned to leave his room since his arrival, and must have all his meals carried up to him by one of the serving wenches."

I saw Philip's hand waver as it conveyed more food to his mouth, and my head jerked up.

"A stranger?" I demanded. "In the village?"

Village was perhaps too dignified a description of Trenowth, through which we had passed at first light that morning. A cluster of cottages grouped around church and hostelry served those families who worked on the manor but did not live in the house itself. The hamlet was set back from the water's edge on a spit of land embraced by the sheltering arm of a small tributary of the river. It had looked prosperous enough in the rosy light of dawn, and plainly benefited from the protection of Sir Peveril and his lady.

Father Anselm must have heard the note of alarm in my voice because he looked surprised and a little curious.

"I admit we are isolated here, and out of the mainstream of events, but strangers are not unknown, as you and your master bear witness. And with the news which reached us yesterday, that the Earl of Oxford has taken St.

Michael's Mount, I should imagine that we may expect some coming and going of authority even in this backwater."

Philip had cleared his mouth by now and recovered his self-control. He kicked me sharply under the table.

"You are quite right, Father. Such a serious event is bound to make much traffic on the roads. This haughty gentleman staying at the inn sounds as though he might well be about the King's business." He deftly changed the conversation, deflecting the priest's interest with a query that took my breath away. "Will you be hearing confessions before you leave us?"

"Of course, my son." Father Anselm was immediately reminded of his parish duties. "For all those who wish to make them, I shall be in the chapel after supper."

I could not imagine Philip Underdown wishing to cleanse his soul, but I could appreciate the sleight of hand by which he had made good my blunder. Too much interest shown in the stranger lodging at the ale-house could be reported to the landlord, who, in his turn, might reveal our presence to his guest. Personally, I had very little hope of the fact being kept a secret for any length of time, and if the visitor were indeed our gentleman of Buckfast Abbey he must already have a pretty good idea of our refuge. But he might also be a perfectly innocent traveller, and until I had confirmed his identity by some careful reconnaissance on the morrow, it would be as well to allay Father Anselm's curiosity and to curb his obvious propensity to gossip.

I glanced around the table. Apart from the priest, Philip and myself, the only other people present were Janet Overy, the steward, two of the little kitchen-maids, who slept in the kitchen at nights, snug on straw pallets by the warmth of the fire, and Isobel and Edgar Warden, who were housed in the servants' quarters along with the housekeeper and Alwyn. Everyone else had homes in the village and would walk up to the house each morning as soon as the gates were open. I caught Janet Overy's eye and looked away quickly. Only she, except my companion and myself, had realized the possible significance of the stranger's presence at the inn because I had told her the whole story, and that indiscretion I had to keep secret from Philip at any cost: I could weather his anger, but not his scorn. Of the rest, Alwyn plainly knew too little to scent any danger, Isobel Warden kept her eyes sullenly on her plate—the badge of her husband's wrath showing in a dark bruise on one side of her face—while Edgar was preoccupied with his own thoughts, none of them happy ones, judging by the venomous glances he kept darting at Philip.

When the meal was at last finished and cleared away, Father Anselm said that he would hear confessions as soon as possible, as the October evenings were drawing in and he wished to get back to the presbytery before twilight. He bustled off across the courtyard to the chapel, which was situated in the corner, between the laundry and the great chamber.

I grinned and hissed in Philip's ear: "The biter bit. I'm afraid you have no choice but to go first." We were standing at the kitchen door, looking out at the thin veil of blue dusk which was beginning to shroud the buildings. I added on a more serious note: "This stranger, do you think he's our attacker?"

"My attacker!" was the abrasive answer. "That's why I've given you the letter. D'you have it safe?" I nodded and he went on: "It may be that we *were* followed after all. But we saw no one, and I'm inclined to doubt it. We are beginning to look for trouble where none exists and jump at our own shadows. You would have had the priest agog with curiosity but for my timely intervention." He said on an ugly note: "And now thanks to your stupidity I'm committed to making my confession, something I've avoided doing these many years." He laughed mirthlessly. "I could tell a tale which would make the poor man die of fright, but I shan't. What's the point? No penance he could give me would wipe away my sins. When I die, I'm going straight to Hell."

CHAPTER
10

It had been one of those pearled, iridescent evenings when the sky seemed to have sucked all the colour from the earth into one vast lake of shimmering whiteness in the heavens. But when I emerged from the chapel, the day, surely one of the longest of my life, was drawing to its close. Torches were being lit, licking the growing darkness with bright tongues of flame. I had been the last to make my confession, and Father Anselm followed me out, making his hurried farewells to Janet Overy and the steward, who bolted and barred the great gates after him, the housekeeper finally locking the wicket door on the left-hand side.

Philip was waiting for me, a sardonic grin on his face. "Cleansed and purged," he said, laughing. "Two Hail Mary's and I'm as good as new. How easy it is to fool these priests."

"But not God," I answered quietly, expecting the vials of his scorn to be poured upon my head.

But instead, his features were wiped clean of all expression and he made no reply. We walked the few steps to the great chamber door, both of us ready for bed, even though it was still early. The housekeeper and the steward called good night and returned to the kitchen, no doubt to chat and drink mulled ale until they, too, felt sleepy. I again felt a stab of guilt when I thought of the revelations I had made to Janet Overy. What, after all, did I know of her? I sighed. The Duke should never have placed his trust in me. I was not cut out for such a devious and underhanded business. Once more, I was tempted to make a clean breast of my indiscretion to Philip, and once more my courage failed me.

We mounted the staircase and entered our room at the end of the short corridor. I laid my cudgel down alongside the truckle-bed and went to the window to shut it. As I leaned out, I cast an anxious glance around, but all seemed quiet, and at the same moment the light finally trembled and died, turning cold and ashen under a darkening sky. I secured the wooden shutter, then closed the window from inside. As I pushed it to, it squeaked slightly on its iron hinges. I sat down on the edge of my bed and pulled off my boots. Philip had already removed his and was unlacing his jerkin.

"You think I was a fool to come here, don't you?" he asked abruptly.

I was startled. It was the first time in the five days we had known one another that he had shown any interest in my opinion, or indeed intimated that I should have one.

"I think we should have done as well to remain in Plymouth," I answered cautiously. "We had as much protection there as here, and you would have known as soon as the *Falcon* put into harbour."

There was silence for a moment, before he said with suppressed violence: "I cannot bear to be cooped up! It frets me to be in a confined space for very long." He stumbled slightly over "frets" and it occurred to me that he had almost used the word "frightens." He forced a laugh. "Folly, of course, but I get nightmares about being chained up in the dark."

I could see that he immediately regretted this admission, and realized that he had made it as a sort of aftermath to his confession to the priest. I said quickly, to put him at his ease: "I, too, have bad dreams at times, usually the consequence of too much ale or sour bread. And you thought that here, at least, we should have the run of the house and not be confined to one room, as at the Turk's Head."

He nodded, apparently relieved that I had made light of his weakness. "I heard of Trenowth Manor some years ago, one summer when my brother and I were working the hamlets and villages on the Devon side of the river, and I came across the Tamar to see if Sir Peveril had any valuable piece of jewellery or silver he might wish to sell. It was the time of Princess Margaret's marriage to the Duke of Burgundy, and many of the lesser gentry were finding it hard to raise enough money in order to ingratiate themselves with a suitable wedding present."

"And did he?"

Philip gave a dry laugh. "I did not even gain access to the courtyard on that occasion, but was sent about my business by Alwyn—who obviously has no recollection of the incident."

"Just as well, since you had to convince him that you are a friend of his master." I ran my fingers over the stubble on my chin. "What exactly did you tell him?"

He yawned cavernously and stretched his arms above his head until the bones cracked. "As little as possible. That I am an agent for the Government, that I need asylum for a few days, and that my friend Sir Peveril, as a true adherent of the House of York, would wish me to stay here. So now, all I have to do is to keep myself amused for a week. That shouldn't be difficult."

"If you're thinking of Isobel Warden—" I began, but he interrupted me with a vicious snap of his fingers.

"How I entertain myself is my affair, so keep your nose out of it. It's your job to see that nothing happens to me, no more. I can look after myself when it comes to women." He gave an ugly grin. "God knows, when it comes to jealous husbands I've had sufficient practice."

I saw that he was in no mood to be reasonable, so I decided to say nothing further for the time being. Indeed, I had no energy left for argument. Our journeying of last night and the events of today had made me very tired. I was now stripped down to my shirt and hose and suggested that we get to sleep. Philip was agreeable, so I crossed to the chest against the wall to blow out the candle. As I stooped to do so, I noticed that someone had placed a small nosegay of daisies alongside the candlestick, and in the middle of the bunch was the stem of knotgrass. I knew it for the same one I had thrown away earlier because it was dry and limp and shrivelled.

I must have made a noise of some sort—a quick intake of breath or a murmur of dismay—for Philip asked sharply: "What's the matter?"

I thought swiftly. Better by far to let him rest soundly tonight and delay telling him about my find until the morning.

"Nothing," I said. "A drop of wax from the candle fell on my hand, that's all."

I dropped the flowers down between the wall and the side of the chest and returned to bed, pulling the blankets up around my chin, but the discovery worried me. I lay staring into the darkness, full of uneasiness and foreboding. Who had rescued the stem of knotgrass from the courtyard and taken the trouble to place it in our room?

What was its significance to Philip? And why had whoever it was picked the daisies? Added to these worries was the memory of my dream; although I comforted myself with the belief that its message was not necessarily of an event which had to happen, but a warning of something which might be prevented. Who was the stranger at the ale-house in the village? My mind was whirling.

Philip called softly: "Roger!"

"What?" My tone was abrupt. I had just begun to doze and I was irritated at having been awakened.

"I want you to keep watch outside the door tonight. I'll feel happier. If anyone tried to get in, he'll have to get past you first and you can raise the alarm."

If I had had all my wits about me I might have protested, or smelt a rat. But finding the knotgrass had disturbed me. I pushed back the covers and swung my feet to the floor.

"Mind you lock the door behind me, then." I put on my jerkin for warmth, made certain that my pouch, containing the letter, was safely bestowed with the rest of my belongings, and picked up my mattress and blankets. I also bent down for my cudgel, but decided against it. If I were attacked in the dark, it would be too unwieldy a weapon with which to defend myself in the confined space of the corridor. I tucked my knife into my belt instead.

A few moments later, having settled my mattress and myself on the stone flags of the passageway, I heard Philip turn the key and then remove it from the lock as an added precaution. After that, silence descended. I covered myself once more with the blankets and tried to keep awake.

It was, of course, impossible. I dozed, woke and dozed again. Eventually, I fell into a troubled sleep and a jumble of nonsensical dreams. Then, suddenly, I found myself sitting bolt upright, my ears straining. All was quiet. I pressed my ear against the keyhole. Silence reigned . . .

My heart began to beat a little faster. The silence, surely, was too profound. Philip Underdown was a man who snored, as I had learned to my cost during our nights spent in the same room at Buckfast Abbey and the Turk's Head. And why had I said yes so readily to his suggestion that I sleep outside the door? I had been all kinds of a fool ever to agree to it, I could see that now. I called through the keyhole: "Philip!"

There was no reply. I called again, louder, but there was still no answer. At last, after several more attempts, I threw caution to the wind and shouted his name, at the same time hammering loudly on the door. The noise I was making should have awakened the dead, and I was thankful that we were housed on the opposite side of the courtyard from the servants. Frantically, I lifted and rattled the latch, but of course it was useless. The door was locked from within. Cursing myself for the greatest idiot unhung, I clapped one eye to the keyhole, but was unable to see anything except a paler darkness. I was locked out of the room and something had happened to Philip.

It was then I remembered the knife in my belt and Nicholas Fletcher, one of my fellow novices at Glastonbury. Nicholas, in his green years, had travelled with his mother in a troupe of jugglers and dancers, often thrown into the company of rogues and vagabonds. From one of these he had learned how to pick locks and, in an idle moment, had passed on that knowledge to me. I had never expected to find a use for it, but now I slid the knife from its sheath and inserted the blade into the lock. For a desperate moment, I could not recall exactly what to do, but my retentive memory stood me in good stead and within seconds, I heard the wards slide free. I flung open the door and fairly hurled myself inside the room.

The bed was empty, the covers thrown back, and both the window and the shutter swinging wide on their hinges.

I pushed the leaded glass in its iron frame back against the inner wall and sent the wooden shutter clattering against the outer. My eyes were now accustomed to the dark, and by leaning over the sill I could just make out the damage done to the vine where Philip had used it as a ladder. He had patently gone of his own free will, to keep some appointment or assignation of which I knew nothing. But where? The woods or the river bank were the obvious answers, for there was no way he could re-enter the courtyard without a key to unlock the gate, and that was in the safe-keeping of the steward. I was sure I was right, for apart from being a natural assumption, there was also the memory of my dream . . .

I prayed desperately that I should be in time to prevent its fulfilment. I had congratulated myself this morning for having the sense to recognize the vine as a means of entry into the bedchamber, but I had overlooked the fact that it could equally well be used as a means of escape. And I should have foreseen that possibility as soon as Philip set eyes on Isobel Warden. How Isobel would manage to get free from the locked compound I did not at that moment pause to examine very closely, but the Trenowth manor house was not fortified, and there were undoubtedly many ways of getting in and out after the gates were locked if you knew them. Such considerations, however, could wait. The only thing which concerned me now was to find Philip and bring him back safely to the house.

I turned and felt beside the frame of the truckle-bed for my cudgel, intending to throw it out of the window ahead of me and retrieve it when I reached the ground. But it had gone, and I realized that Philip must have taken it. Cursing under my breath, I clambered on to the window-sill, leant sideways, managed to get a grip on the vine and cautiously allowed my legs to swing free until they, too, found a toehold among the branches. Minutes later, my feet came into contact with solid earth and I knew that I was down. With a quick, whispered prayer of thankfulness, I trod across the grass to the track leading to the mill, the saw-pit, the river and the village, set amongst its surrounding swathe of trees.

A freshening breeze stirred the branches which arched and interlaced above me. I could feel the unevenness of the path beneath my feet and hear the scufflings of some small, nocturnal animal as it hurried to safety beneath a tangle of briers and bushes. My apprehension was turning to fear for Philip's safety as I padded slowly forward, my feet making no sound, except for the occasional snapping of a twig. I raised my eyes for a moment, glimpsing the crescent moon riding cold and high between the gathering clouds. The weather was changing, an autumnal squall blowing in from the sea.

Below me, where the bank dropped sheer and the bushes thinned, I could see a glint of the Tamar. Several times I stopped to glance back over my shoulder, listening intently for any noise which might indicate Philip's where-abouts, although common sense suggested that I should find him with Isobel Warden among the long grass border-ing the river. I was conscious of a prickle of sweat across my shoulder-blades.

I paused at each twist and bend of the path, scanning the darkness ahead. Once an owl swooped low across my line of vision, gliding silently from one perch to another. The sudden movement startled me and I stood stock-still, my breath coming short and fast, my heart pounding in my breast. Then, carefully, I resumed my walk, aware that I had almost completed the descent, and in a few more mo-ments I was standing level with the river. There was a break in the trees and I was able to make out the broad expanse of water stretching to the farther bank, silvered fleetingly with moonlight.

I called softly: "Philip! Philip, are you there?" Receiving no answer, I prowled warily forward, the tall grasses reaching half way up my legs. The owl hooted in the trees behind me . . .

The toe of my left boot stubbed against some large object lying half hidden amongst the vegetation. The hairs on the nape of my neck rose in horror, and I glanced down just as the fragile crescent moon emerged once more from behind the clouds, allowing me to make out the shape of a body. "Mary, Mother of God," I prayed fervently, "don't let it be Philip." On trembling legs, I forced myself to stoop and peer more closely.

He was lying face down. I put out a hand and touched the back of his head, then withdrew it quickly. I felt the wet stickiness on my fingers which could only mean blood. Philip's skull had been beaten in. I had broken my dream.

I sat back on my heels, trying to stop the shaking which seemed to possess every part of my body. My brain had ceased to function and I have no idea how long I stayed like that, without any awareness of the passage of time, devoid of all sensations. All too soon, however, the numbness passed, plunging me into a whirlpool of conflicting and panic-stricken emotions. But gradually these too were brought under control and I forced myself to try and think clearly. I crossed myself, then began feeling the earth around the body, searching for anything which might possibly have been dropped by the murderer and so give me a lead to his identity.

I found it, but it was not what I had hoped for or expected. With mounting horror my fingers identified the boles and knot-holes of my own stout cudgel, and one end of it was still wet with blood. My mind raced, darting frantically from side to side like a squirrel in a cage. Philip had brought it with him to his assignation as a protection against attack, but it had been wrenched from him and used to kill him. So much was clear to me, but what was even clearer was that if I left it here and raised the alarm, I myself might come under suspicion. And in order not to betray the Duke of Gloucester's trust in me completely, I should now have to take Philip's place aboard the *Falcon* and carry King Edward's letter to the Breton court. I must return immediately to the house, taking my "Plymouth Cloak" with me, and leave Philip's body to be discovered by someone else.

But Philip had come to meet another person, and I had no doubt in my mind that it was Isobel Warden. So what had happened to her? Had she changed her mind and not kept her assignation? Had she, on the other hand, been present when Philip was murdered and seen who did it? A moment's swift consideration, however, dismissed this second notion: surely she too would have been killed had that happened. And had she been nearby, yet not close enough to have been noticed by the attacker, then she would be unable to identify him because of the enveloping darkness. In any case, she was unlikely to come forward as a witness, an action which would involve an explanation as to how she came to be abroad in the middle of the night with Philip Underdown. No, even if she were still lurking, terrified, among the trees somewhere, I had nothing to fear from her if I practised my deception.

Rising slowly and cautiously to my feet, I picked up my cudgel and carried it the few feet to the river's edge, the bank in this spot being no more than two feet high. By lying flat on my stomach I was able to trail the end stained with blood in the water, holding it in the swiftly flowing tide. That done, I once again got up and, in a sweat of fear, glancing continuously behind me, retraced my steps to the house and re-entered the way I had left it.

CHAPTER
11

 Once back in the room I had shared with Philip, I closed the shutter and secured the window from inside. I made two unsuccessful attempts to light the candle, the first time letting the tinder-box slip through my trembling fingers, the second failing to make sufficient spark between steel and flint to ignite the tinder. On the third occasion, however, I managed to produce a flame and soon had the candle burning. After that, I was forced to pause for several moments, kneeling beside the chest while the strength returned to my legs, and only then was I able to open the door and retrieve my mattress and blankets from the passageway.

I hunted around until I found the key where Philip had dropped it, on top of the table alongside his "all-night." This had not been touched, the jug of ale still full, the small loaf of bread still uneaten. I realized suddenly that in spite of everything, I was desperately hungry. I had not broken my fast since supper, and not even abject fear and panic could quell my appetite. But first I must make sure

that the lock of the door still worked; that I had not damaged it beyond use with my inexpert lock-picking. It was
almost with disbelief that I heard the wards slide smoothly
home, and blessed Nicholas Fletcher for his careful tuition.
I sat down on the edge of Philip's cold mattress and started
eating.

Until I had satisfied my hunger and slaked my thirst, I
refused to face the shadows gibbering for attention on the
fringes of my mind. I was cold and hot by turns, appalled
by what had happened. And angry, too; angry at my own
incredible simplicity and stupidity, which had allowed
Philip to play a trick on me which should not have
deceived a schoolboy; but angry, also, with Philip's own
irresponsibility, which had led him to risk his mission and
his life for a clandestine meeting with a woman. But I must
not permit my emotions to override all other considerations. Before daylight came, and the inevitable discovery
of the body, there were matters I had to sort out and dispositions to make. For that, I needed nourishment.

The bread and ale, eaten to the last crumb and drained
to the final dreg, did their work and made me feel a little
better. My head cleared somewhat, and I proceeded to do
what I should have done immediately on returning to the
bedchamber; I checked my belongings to make sure that
King Edward's letter to Duke Francis was still among them.
It showed what an innocent I was in this world of plot and
counter-plot that I had not until this moment considered
the possibility that Philip might have been lured from the
room in order for someone to steal what he had been killed
for. The letter was, however, still there, in my own pouch,
wrapped in my bundle beneath the truckle-bed, and I sent
up a heartfelt prayer of gratitude.

Philip's motive for entrusting me with the letter was
now clearer. With one corner of his mind, he had acknowledged the risk he was running with this midnight

assignation. What was it he had said? "*If anything should happen to me, it could be the first thing my attacker would look for about my person.*" There had been a whiff of danger in his nostrils, which he had considered too faint to heed very deeply, but he had made what precaution he could against it. Yet surely he would not have taken the letter with him to a love-tryst with Isobel Warden? He would have left it behind. Even so, he had considered it safer among my belongings than his own . . .

My eyelids were beginning to droop. In spite of the turmoil of my mind and the need to act the innocent when daylight came at last, my body demanded rest. It is the one craving almost impossible to resist, over which we have no control. I have heard of men condemned to the gallows still sleeping soundly on the eve of execution. And I was no exception. Without any later memory of doing so, I lay down on my bed, covered myself with the blankets, and within moments was fast asleep.

No dreams disturbed my slumbers; no nightmares came to carry me on their backs to the gates of some hideous world where horrid fancies lurked, waiting to assume human shape and gather me into their fearful embrace. Rather, I slept deeply and awoke refreshed, conscious that it was morning even before I noticed, beyond the leaded glass, the faint rim of daylight around the shutter. I stretched contentedly, as someone who was at peace with himself and his surroundings, before I turned my head and saw Philip's empty bed. At once, memory came flooding back. I sat upright, starting to sweat, while I tried to convince myself that my experiences of the night had been nothing more than a terrible dream. But it was no use. Philip was dead, murdered, and in order to deflect suspicion from myself I must pretend not to know what had happened until the news was brought by others.

I opened the window inwards and unbarred the shutter, flinging it back against the outer wall. A hazy sunlight lit the chamber, the threatened storm of the night either having passed or come to nothing. It was not as clear and crisp a day as the previous one had been, but the breeze had dropped and the darker clouds dispersed, leaving only a faint, milky whiteness to obscure the sun. I turned back into the room and picked up my cudgel from the floor where I had laid it on my return earlier that morning. Carrying it across to the window, I examined it more closely and was able to see that, in spite of its cleaning in the river, it was still badly discoloured at one end. There were also a few of Philip's dark curly hairs adhering to the wood, and I carefully picked them off before letting them float out of the window. That done, I felt easier in my mind. The discoloration, if noticed, could more simply be explained away, and in any case, only the murderer knew that it was the weapon used to kill Philip Underdown.

The next thing to do was to hide the King's letter about my person, but my belt-pouch was too obvious a place for concealment. After a moment or two, I thought of my jerkin. This was no peasant's garment, made of that rough woollen cloth known in my youth as brocella, but was fashioned from soft leather, and had been given to me by a widow as payment for some goods which I had sold her. She had fallen on hard times since her husband's death, and had been happy to let me exchange my wares for some of his clothes, which were no longer of any use to her. The attraction of the jerkin had been its lining which was made from scarlet, that soft, cochineal-dyed wool normally used for undergarments, a protection against cold in the winter months. Now I proposed using it for another purpose and, taking my knife, I made a slit of several inches in the lining of the front left-hand side, pushing the letter between the wool and the leather. Later, I would ask Janet Overy for a needle and thread to make fast the rent, but in the meantime the paper would be safe enough, dropping as it would to the hem with no danger of falling out or being lost. That done, I put the jerkin on and fastened it at the waist, before using the garderobe at the top of the stairs and proceeding to the kitchen for breakfast. (Here, I must say that "privy" has always been a good enough word for me, but some people have tender sensibilities and prefer the Norman French.)

I crossed the courtyard warily, every sense alert for any sign of commotion, but as yet there was none. The gates stood open and a steady stream of servants and manor dependants passed in and out. Smoke poured from the hole in the bakery roof and steam issued from the laundry, where a cauldron of water heated slowly over the fire. I entered the kitchen, aware that the morning was already some way advanced and that it was probably nearer eight o'clock than seven. This assumption was borne out by the fact that two of the kitchen-maids were scouring the pots and pans used to cook the various breakfast dishes, and because Janet Overy turned a frowning face towards me.

"You and your master are late this morning," she grumbled and nodded towards the table. "Sit down, sit down!" She picked up a wooden bowl. "I'll get you some porridge. And Agnes!" She addressed one of the maids. "Give Roger Chapman a mazer of ale." She went on, filling the bowl with gruel: "And where's your master, eh? If he lies abed much longer he'll get nothing to eat until dinner. I can't keep food hot and the girls idling about here all morning. They've other work to do, and so have I."

She seemed harassed, and I wished she had been in better mood. It would have been easier to practise my deception. However, there was no help for it and I said as calmly as I could: "But I thought Master Underdown had already eaten. He was not in his bed when I awoke and I imagined he had risen early. You . . . You have not seen him then?"

"No, I have not," she answered testily. "And it seems to me a great pity that he should have gone wandering off about the manor before breaking his fast." She placed the bowl of porridge before me, adding on a gentler note: "Perhaps when you have finished eating, you would find him, if he has not come back by then." As though suddenly ashamed of her ill-humour, she smiled and patted my shoulder. "Sorry, lad. It's not your fault that Master Underdown is not here. But all has gone awry this morning. I myself overslept and was late in rousing Alwyn to unlock the gates. And when he did get them open, we found another visitor at our door, another mouth to feed." She jerked her head in the direction of the kitchen fire, where I became aware for the first time of a man's figure seated on a stool, hunched forward, his hands extended towards the flames for warmth.

There was something familiar about the man's back, but before I had time to speculate on who he was, he rose from the stool and I was able to see him clearly. Short and stocky, with light sandy hair, straggling beard, weather-beaten countenance and a pair of very bright blue eyes, he was instantly recognizable.

"You!" I gasped. "What in heaven's name are you doing here? And how did you find us?"

It was Silas Bywater.

He brought his stool over to the table and sat down beside me, sucking and picking at his teeth, obviously having fed well and enjoyed his breakfast.

"Oh, you weren't difficult to find," he said, "not for

someone like me, who has friends in Plymouth. It didn't take me long to discover you and Master Underdown had been staying at the Turk's Head. And the landlord didn't deny it, when I put it to him. But he said you'd left and he didn't know where you'd gone." Silas laughed. "Of course I knew he was lying."

"When did you reach Plymouth?" I asked. My mind was racing, trying to assess what the presence of Silas Bywater in the neighbourhood meant. If he had been waiting outside the gates this morning, he had plainly been in the vicinity of the manor, even within its pale, last night. Was he Philip's murderer, and not the unknown traveller at the inn, after all? Had he been the man I had seen lurking in the shadows on Sutton harbour quay? There were so many questions and as yet no answers. I had, moreover, to school my features into near indifference, as though his movements were of little importance. I prayed that someone would come soon with news of Philip's death. I found it difficult to dissemble.

"Towards dusk on Saturday," he said in reply to my question. "I got a lift from a man carting peat as far as Plympton Priory. I spent Friday night there and finished my journey the following day on foot, reaching home late in the afternoon, so I made no inquiries for you until the Sunday. Not that inquiries were really necessary." He grinned and stroked his beard. "I knew where Master Underdown would be. Where he always lodged when he was in Plymouth, with his crony John Penryn."

I said slowly: "So you were in the town on Saturday night and knew where to find us. You didn't, perhaps, attempt to break into Master Underdown's bedchamber with a view to finishing what you had tried to accomplish, but failed to do at Buckfast Abbey?"

He sent me a sidelong glance, showing the whites of his eyes like a nervous horse. "I don't know what you're talking about," he answered. "I've come after Philip Underdown for one reason only, to prise out of him some of the money he once promised and has never paid me."

"You still haven't told me how you traced us here. You say John Penryn denied all knowledge of our whereabouts."

Silas Bywater shrugged. "If you want to leave a city secretly, at night, you should control your horses better. If one gives voice, it attracts attention. A friend of mind saw men and horses passing her window well after curfew, and judged by their general direction that they were on the road to the ferry. The ferryman is another old friend of mine and confirmed that he conveyed two men and their mounts across the Tamar in the dead hours of night when honest citizens should be sleeping in their beds. He also told me that once on the other side, his passengers rode north. I spent all yesterday following in your footsteps and making inquiries at every house I passed. I knew that if Philip Underdown was working this side of the river, he would be holed up somewhere, although God knows I didn't expect to find him housed as well as this! I spent last night sleeping under a hedge, and only came to the gate this morning to beg some breakfast before carrying on with my search. When you walked in just now and I realized you and Master Underdown must be staying here, I could hardly believe my eyes. But then I thought: Why not? He always had the nerve of the devil!" Silas Bywater shifted on his stool and turned to face me, looking me squarely in the face for the first time. "You're his new partner, are you? Taken the place of his brother? Strange, you don't look like the sort of young man to be mixed up in Philip Underdown's business."

I stared at him stupidly for a moment or two before suddenly understanding. Of course, Silas Bywater had no means of knowing that Philip had changed his occupation after that last ill-fated voyage of the *Speedwell*. He still thought him engaged in the business of trading and slaving, and imagined me to be his accomplice. But that did not mean he was innocent of Philip's murder. If he had come across him by chance last night, the desire for revenge might have overwhelmed him. He could well have seized or picked up the cudgel and bludgeoned Philip to death before stopping to think what he was doing.

At this point Janet Overy, who had been instructing the kitchen-maids in the making of a beef and vegetable pottage, left the cooking-bench at the far end of the kitchen and came across to the table.

"I cannot keep the porridge hot any longer," she told me briskly. "I need the chimney crane to hang the stew-pot on, so your master will have to go hungry until dinner. If you find him, tell him so." She glanced at Silas Bywater. "And you, my man, you're welcome to stay and share another meal with us if you're so minded." She studied him thoughtfully. "Your face is familiar. Have we met somewhere before, or am I mistaken?"

Silas returned her stare. "Not to my knowledge, Mistress. I've never seen you before that I remember."

I caught the housekeeper's eye and said with meaning: "This is Silas Bywater, a former friend of Master Underdown."

I saw her rack her brains for a second or two before memory grasped the significance of the name. "Of course." She smiled. "Many years ago now, when I lived on the other side of the river, I used to visit Plymouth market once a month for supplies. I recall seeing you in Master Underdown's company and hearing your name. You were a sea-captain in those days, unless I'm mistaken."

"And still am, when the work offers." Silas grinned

complacently, pleased no doubt to feel that he was a well-known enough figure in his native town to be pointed out and his face remembered by a good-looking woman, even if she was by now growing a little long in the tooth.

I rose to my feet. "I'll go and look for my master," I said reluctantly, disliking thoroughly the deception I was forcing myself to practise.

"I'll come with you." Silas Bywater also got up, adding over his shoulder to Janet Overy: "I'll stay for dinner, thank you kindly, Mistress. I have some unfinished business I want to discuss with Master Underdown." He followed me outside into the hazy sunshine of the courtyard, saying curiously: "So he's your master, eh?" He looked at me appraisingly. "That makes more sense. He'd need a good, strong, healthy, young bodyguard like you to keep him safe from all the people who wish him harm. And from what you let drop just now, there's been someone wishing him ill both at Buckfast and at Plymouth." He laughed nastily. "That explains the secret midnight flight. But whoever it was, it wasn't me. I want Philip Underdown alive, leastways until I get what the lying bastard owes me. I warned him that once I'd found him again, I wouldn't easily let go."

He sounded genuine enough, but then it was in his interest to do so were he the murderer, because soon the body would be found and there must surely be an inquiry.

I walked towards the open gate, conscious of him hard on my heels. We had almost reached the shadowed arch-way when I heard the noise of wheels on the track beyond and voices shouting and hallooing for attention. Moments later, the cart used to carry logs up from the saw-pit, attended by the sawyer and his assistant whom I had seen the previous day, rattled over the cobbled underpass and came to a standstill in the middle of the courtyard, the flanks of the horse between the shafts sweating and heaving, the poor animal having been driven at a faster pace than he was normally accustomed to. But there were no logs in the cart today; only the sprawled, dead body of Philip Underdown.

CHAPTER

12

 In the end, it was Silas Bywater who first stepped up to the cart.

"Knifed," he said succinctly. "Through the heart."

"What? You must—" I had been going to say: "You must be mistaken," but I cut my words off short. I stepped forward to see for myself.

Philip was lying on his back, heaved unceremoniously on to the boards by the sawyer and his assistant, the strong features, beneath their coating of dirt and grass stains, waxen and somehow diminished by death. The eyes were half shut, the heavy lids concealing any final expression of surprise or horror at his approaching fate. The knees of his hose and the toes of his boots were caked with earth, where he had lain face downwards throughout the long hours of darkness on the water-logged river bank. The front of his jerkin, too, was discoloured, but mixed with the mud were runnels of a more sinister, rusty brown, which stemmed from the handle of a knife driven into his chest up to the hilt and firmly embedded in tissue and muscle.

"The back of 'is 'ead's been stove in, too," the sawyer said with relish. "Whoever done it, made a proper job of it, I reckon."

A picture of what had actually happened to Philip was beginning to form in my mind as I realized that the knife might not have killed him. I felt sure that it had been the murderer's intention to stab him to death, but the aim had gone awry in the blackness, and Philip, although felled, had still been breathing. He had fallen forward, the knife in his body, and the killer had then looked for a means to finish his handiwork. My cudgel, which Philip had taken with him, must have slipped from his hand and been used to batter in his skull, thus completing the grisly business. I leaned a little closer to examine the shaft of the knife, but it was plain bone, undistinguished by any markings, and might have been bought at any cutler's shop or market stall in the country.

By this time, the rest of the manor servants, those within earshot, had become aware that something un-towards had happened. Mistress Overy and the two kitchen-maids emerged from the kitchen, the laundress and her helpers materialized through the clouds of steam issuing from the laundry door, the baker appeared, his apron covered in flour and his hands caked with dough, while Alwyn hurried across the courtyard from the main hall, his long dark-blue gown flapping about thin ankles. Seconds later, Isobel Warden came out of the servants' living quarters, the coils of red hair glinting in the sunlight and immodestly uncovered by a matron's hood. She wore a dress of dark green wool which reflected the colour of her eyes and did nothing to conceal the curves of her splendid figure. Philip might well have thought her worth taking any risk for.

For a long moment there was silence, while they all gathered round the cart to peer at its contents. I could almost see their first rejection of the evidence of their eyes, slowly replaced by dawning acceptance and mounting horror. One of the laundry girls screamed and gave way to strong hysterics; Alwyn visibly blenched; the two little kitchen-maids clung together for support; and the baker wiped his forehead with the back of his hand, leaving a trail of flour behind it. The two seemingly least affected were the housekeeper and Isobel Warden, the former having had enough tragedy in her life to be undismayed by this present demonstration of the harshness of fate, the latter unmoved for reasons I hardly dared guess at. Had Isobel known what to expect before she approached the cart? The lovely face, with its creamy skin and delicate pallor, gave away no secrets.

"Is he dead?" asked Alwyn, more to break his silence than from any doubts on the matter.

"Both back and front," the sawyer replied, revealing himself to be a man with a morbid sense of humour. He added for the benefit of those not yet in the know: "The back of 'is skull's been cracked open."

The steward took a deep breath. In the absence of his master and mistress, the decision of what to do next rested with him and he found himself momentarily at a loss as to how to proceed. The violent death of one who claimed to be a friend of Sir Peveril under Sir Peveril's own roof was plainly a serious matter, and one that he felt ill-equipped to deal with.

"We'd better send to London to let Sir Peveril know what's happened. Meanwhile, someone must ride to Launceston Castle and fetch the Sheriff's officer from the garrison." Alwyn looked around the circle of faces. "Thomas Sawyer, you can do that. Get John Groom to saddle the grey mare when he returns from exercising the horses. If you leave within the hour and ride hard, you should be there by midday and return with the Sheriff's officer before nightfall. Were you the one that found him?"

Thomas Sawyer nodded, pleased with his sudden importance and delighted at the prospect of a day's freedom from the saw-pit and a chance to delegate all work to his assistant. "I was going for a walk along the river bank to stretch my legs. It's cramping work, standing in that pit for hours on end," he added defensively. "I fell over 'im. 'E was lying face down in the long grass by the water's edge. Almost nigh impossible to see 'im from the path, I'd reckon."

"Yes, well, we'd better carry the body indoors," Alwyn instructed. "We'll set up a trestle in the great hall and lay it in there. Thomas, you and young Gerard can see to that. By which time John Groom should have returned with the horses and you can be off to Launceston. Then, Gerard lad, you go back down to the village and round up the rest of the men. Tell them what's happened. Colin and Ned are working on the east fence with Edgar Warden." He turned to the rest of us with a sweeping gesture of one arm. "Come! Let's go indoors. There's no point lingering outside, and I think, Mistress Overy, a measure of strong ale for everyone would not come amiss. On second thoughts, perhaps wine would be more appropriate, and I'm sure Sir Peveril would not object in the circumstances. You have the key to the buttery."

"I'll see to it at once." Janet Overy swung briskly on her heel and shepherded the kitchen- and laundry-maids back into the house, the laundress and baker following behind, neither willing to let a measure of free wine go begging. And any excuse to break off work was always welcome.

As we entered the kitchen, I caught at the steward's sleeve, drawing him to one side. The mention of John

Groom and the horses had presented me with another problem.

"Master Underdown told you something of the business he was on," I said in a low voice. "I shall now have to finish it for him. Can I stable his horse here until I can contact those who will have it collected?"

Alwyn looked faintly surprised. "It will remain here. It was certainly the most valuable item in Master Underdown's possession at the time of his death, and as that death has taken place within the pale of Trenowth Manor, the animal now belongs to Sir Peveril." He raised his eyebrows at my obvious bewilderment. "That is Cornish manorial law," he explained. "Is it not the same in England?"

"Not to my knowledge," I answered drily. "But I am not well versed in legal matters. The monks at Glastonbury taught me to read and write, but the acquisition of property was not considered a fit subject for novices, although no doubt I should have learned more had I stayed long enough to rise in the Church hierarchy." Alwyn seemed more than a little shocked by such blatant cynicism and I decided that I had said enough. My tongue would get me into trouble one of these days, I thought. And the problem of what to do about Philip's fleabitten grey had been resolved for me, if not in quite the manner I had envisaged. I directed Alwyn's attention to Mistress Overy, who had reentered the kitchen carrying two large leather bottles.

These were duly opened and wine poured for everyone present. Several minutes later, Thomas Sawyer and his assistant Gerard came in to claim their share and to report that the body was now lying on a trestle in the great hall and awaiting the ministrations of the women.

"Someone should inform the parish priest," I reminded the steward, "that we shall be in need of his services. Fortunately, Master Underdown, like the rest of us, made his confession last night and was given absolution. Therefore there can be no argument as to the state of his soul at the time of death." Even as I spoke, I wondered secretly about the truth of those words; but as far as Father Anselm was concerned he could bury Philip with a clear conscience.

Alwyn nodded. "Thomas, you can call at the priest's house on your way and tell him what has happened. It being St. Faith's Day, Father Anselm will be holding a special Mass, so if he cannot see you himself, leave word with his housekeeper or a neighbour. Now, if you've finished your wine, be off with you to Launceston. There's no time to lose if you and the Sheriff's officer are to be here by nightfall."

The sawyer grumbled a little at being forced to hurry, but he was too pleased by the prospect of a day's freedom to do more than mutter a single imprecation beneath his breath; a sop to his self-esteem. He would have thought poorly of himself had he not made some token of resistance against authority. He drained the last dregs of wine, replaced his cup on the table and squared his shoulders.

"I'm off, then," he said. "John Groom returned from exercising the horses ten minutes since. I'll be saddled up and ready to go before you can say 'Knife!' " The infelicity of this last remark struck him like a blow and he reddened. "Well . . . God be with you all. I'll return as soon as I can."

"And I'll tell the others what has happened," Gerard said, suddenly recollecting his earlier instructions from the steward. He slid out of the kitchen in Thomas's wake to escape a reprimand.

Alwyn stared after his retreating back with a measure of strong disapproval before returning to the disagreeable job awaiting his attention. He looked at Janet Overy. "Will you and one of the girls see to the laying out?"

The kitchen- and laundry-maids, whose previous distress had simmered down to a nervous, wide-eyed whispering among themselves, immediately showed every sign of boiling over again into hysterics. The housekeeper silenced them with a swift reassurance.

"Isobel will help me, won't you, my dear?"

The younger woman, who had hardly touched her wine and was sitting at the kitchen table watching us all with a kind of bored detachment, answered indifferently: "If you wish it."

"I do wish it." Janet Overy spoke briskly, trying to bring a little normality back into a situation fraught with horror and suspicion. "We'll go at once. There's no reason for delay." She turned to begin her preparations, pouring hot water from the pan over the fire into a big earthenware bowl, and directing one of the kitchen-maids to the linenpress for a clean nightgown, sheet and some rags. When these were assembled, she nodded again at Isobel Warden. "Bring the linen, I'll carry the bowl." She added: "We shall be a while. I suggest the rest of you, if Alwyn Steward is agreeable, get back to work as quickly as possible. You will feel the better for it."

The younger members of the household were inclined to doubt this wisdom, but the laundress ordered her assistants' return to the laundry in a voice which brooked no argument, and the baker said reluctantly that he must look to his bread or the loaves would all be burnt. The two kitchen-maids, under Alwyn's eagle eye, had perforce to resume their duties, both a trifle unsteady on their feet from the effects of the wine. They went to the opposite end of the kitchen and began chopping vegetables for dinner with an abandon which made me anxious for the safety of their fingers.

I laid a hand on the steward's arm, hoping to draw him away from Silas Bywater's vicinity for some private discourse, but at that moment Edgar Warden entered the kitchen, two other men—the Colin and Ned named earlier by Alwyn—close behind him. The swarthy features were taut with suspicion, as though he feared a trick was being played on him.

"What's this nonsense young Gerard's been telling us?" he demanded truculently. "There's still a lot of work to be done on that boundary fence today. If the lad's been playing one of his tricks on us, I'll skin him alive!"

There was muttered agreement from his two companions, but Alwyn quickly held up his hand.

"I'm afraid what Gerard told you is true. Our guest, Master Underdown, was murdered last night, down by the river bank. I've sent for the Sheriff's officer from Launceston Castle. Until his arrival, there's nothing further we can do. Mistress Overy is laying out the body now in the great hall."

I had been observing Edgar Warden closely from the moment he came in, because, along with the unknown stranger who had stopped at the Trenowth inn, he was one of my chief suspects for Philip's murder. And if Philip had indeed had a tryst with the beautiful Isobel, and they had been surprised by her husband, there was no doubt in my mind about the latter's reaction. True, they would have been equally matched in size and weight, but they would not have been meeting in fair fight. My guess was that if Edgar were the murderer, he had somehow got wind of his wife's intended assignation and lain in wait. He had then confronted Philip, knife in hand, and struck in such blind fury that his aim had been untrue. Philip had fallen to his knees, but still alive, only to be bludgeoned to death by the cudgel he had dropped.

This version of the murder could also hold good for the unknown stranger, the hired assassin of the Woodvilles or the Tudors, and I had to keep an open mind. There was, in addition, a third possibility in the shape of Silas Bywater, watching us all with those bright, bird-like eyes, darting from one to the other and sharp with cunning. He had sworn to get his revenge on Philip; and although Philip was unquestionably more good to him alive than dead, Silas would not be the first man to kill in a fit of uncontrollable anger. There was also the possibility that Silas was the person Philip had gone to meet, although I did not really think so. He would have wasted neither time nor energy climbing out of the bedchamber window in order to tell Silas in secret what he had told him before in the presence of other people. Unless . . . Unless Philip had meant to kill Silas and so end his threats and importuning forever. My head began to swim as I suddenly found myself floundering in a sea of possibilities.

Edgar Warden sat down at the table, Colin and Ned following suit, and Alwyn pushed the bottle still containing wine towards them. He called to one of the kitchen-maids to bring three more mazers and himself poured out when they were brought.

"Here, drink this. Some of Sir Peveril's best, but in the circumstances Mistress Overy and I thought he would not grudge it us."

The bailiff emptied his cup in almost one gulp, then wiped his mouth on the back of his hand. "I can't say I'm sorry that Underdown's dead," he said after a moment's silence, face and voice alike devoid of expression. "What little I saw of him, yesterday, I had no cause to like. A man who had made many enemies in his time, I shouldn't wonder."

"And that's God's truth!" Silas Bywater chimed in unexpectedly from his fireside corner. "You know a rogue when you see one, friend."

"Who's this?" Edgar wanted to know with a jerk of his head in Silas's direction.

"I was ship's captain for Philip Underdown in the old days, trading out of Plymouth. He had others in Bristol and

London, when the Speedwell sailed from those ports, as it did from time to time. And if he treated them as shabbily as he did me and my crew, then he's enemies a-plenty."

"But you're here and Master Underdown's dead," I pointed out dulcetly, and for the first time saw a flicker of fear in those bright blue eyes. "On your own admission, you followed us from Plymouth and were in the neighbourhood of Trenowth last night."

Silas leaped unsteadily to his feet, his hands clenched at his sides. "Here! What are you suggesting?" he demanded.

"I'm suggesting nothing, merely repeating what you told Mistress Overy and myself this morning. And you will no doubt have to account for your presence to the Sheriff's officer when he arrives."

Silas Bywater sat down again slowly, a little white about the mouth. He seemed genuinely taken aback by the realization that he could be implicated in Philip's murder, a fact which might indicate his innocence of the crime, or merely his ability to disguise his true thoughts and emotions. I did not know him well enough to pass judgement, any more than I was able to guess at this juncture whether or not Edgar Warden's indifference was a bluff. I could only wait and see what time and the Sheriff's officer's inquiry revealed between them.

But it was the advent of the Sheriff's officer from Launceston that worried me. If Philip had, as I more than half suspected, been murdered by an agent of the Woodvilles or the Tudors, the Duke of Gloucester would undoubtedly wish the matter to remain a secret, particularly so if the Queen's relatives were involved. An official investigation into the cause of Philip's death could do much harm and might even imperil my own chances of getting the King's letter safely to Duke Francis in Brittany. If, however, I could present the Sheriff's officer on his arrival at Trenowth this evening with the identity of the murderer, or alternatively show him good cause why he should not proceed with an official inquiry into Philip's death, then I could still carry out the Duke's mission. I had failed his trust in me to protect my companion's life, but all was not yet lost, provided I could indeed achieve the well-nigh impossible task that I had set myself.

CHAPTER

13

By the time Janet Overy and Isobel came back to the kitchen from the great hall, having completed their task of laying out the body, the bailiff and his two helpers had finished their wine and returned to their work on Trenowth Manor's eastern fence. Alwyn had also fussily removed himself to make sure that Thomas Sawyer had indeed already left for Launceston Castle and was not indulging in a lengthy gossip with the groom. Silas was still huddled close to the fire, his leathery features deeply grooved with an expression of injured innocence every time I glanced in his direction.

I rose to my feet as the women entered and asked: "Is all well? Can I see him?"

Mistress Overy restored the now empty bowl to its place on a shelf and indicated to Isobel Warden that, for the moment, she had no further use for her services. The girl was not a servant, and although she doubtless helped around the manor when requested, she was primarily the wife of Trenowth's chief retainer after Alwyn and Janet herself.

"Of course all's well," the housekeeper answered, offended. "I've laid out enough bodies before now to know what I'm about." I thought guiltily of her husband and son and cursed my careless tongue. My contrition must have been visible, because she added on a softer note: "But no, you can't see him. The door to the great hall has been locked on Alwyn's orders until the Sheriff's officer arrives tonight, and Alwyn has the key." She eyed me closely. "You look pale and drawn, lad. You'd best sit down again and I'll fetch you more wine. You're taking this hard, even though you didn't like the man."

I saw Silas turn his head curiously at this, and hurriedly assured her that I needed nothing else to drink. "But I'd like to speak to Master Steward if I may."

Janet shook her head doubtfully. "He's busy, and won't take kindly to being disturbed at present. Apart from his ordinary duties, he must despatch someone to London to take news of this unfortunate happening to Sir Peveril and his lady. And preparations must be made to receive the Sheriff's officer when he comes. Which reminds me, a room must be got ready for him. The allocating of guests to rooms is my job, not Alwyn's." She lifted the bunch of keys which hung from her belt and started to sift through them, her mind already intent on domestic duties to the exclusion of almost everything else. Her previous advice to the other servants, to continue with their normal round of chores, seemed to be working wonders in her own case. From her unruffled and practical behaviour it would have been difficult to detect that anything untowards had occurred that morning.

She made briskly for the kitchen door and I followed her outside, into the courtyard. The day had lost its early promise. The sky had grown overcast again as more rain clouds swept in from the sea, piling up dark and menacing on the horizon. The night's faint breeze had returned to disturb the tops of trees visible above the quadrangle of buildings. Autumn was settling over the land in all its variable moods, and October's thin sunshine was no match for its sudden squalls and storms. With each passing day, sea-crossings would become more perilous and the movement of ships more unpredictable. I must be ready and waiting in Plymouth when the Falcon eventually appeared, as I had no doubt it would, released on the King's orders from its watch on St. Michael's Mount. I could afford no delay while the Sheriff's officer made his inquiries into Philip's death.

I caught Janet Overy by the arm as she was about to hurry away. She turned an irritated face towards me.

"Would you or Master Steward have any objections to my asking some questions of the servants on the Manor? And there are inquires I wish to make at the village inn. Would either of you put a rub in my way?"

The housekeeper looked blank, then shrugged. "It's all the same to me, and I can't think that Alwyn would try to prevent you. The sooner this business is cleared up, the better for us all. I think you'd be wiser to wait for the Sheriff's officer, but that's for you to decide. No doubt, after what you told me yesterday, you have suspicions of your own. Nevertheless, don't make any attempt to leave the manor lands. Anyone foolish enough to do that would fall foul of the law and be immediately suspected. The hue and cry would be set after him in no time." She nodded her head in the direction of the kitchen door. "You'd better tell that to your friend, Silas Bywater. He's twitchy since you warned him that he, too, might be thought to be the murderer. Now, I have work to do. I can't stand here talking all day."

She moved purposefully away from me towards the entrance to the great chamber with its staircase to the upper floor, but once again I ran after, and detained, her.

"There's something I've just remembered!"

Her annoyance showed itself plainly this time and she rounded on me with a set and angry face. "In Jesu's name, what now?"

I realized that for all her placid exterior, she was as upset and disturbed by the murder as the rest of us, and that it was only her sense of responsibility to the younger members of the household which made her appear indifferent to it. In her lady's absence, it was up to her to preserve calm and dignity in the face of unforeseen adversity.

"Forgive me," I said, "but there's something I must ask you." I went on quickly, before she could throw off my restraining hand and leave me standing: "Last night, when Master Underdown and I went to bed, I found that someone had placed a bunch of daisies on the chest beside our candlestick, and in the middle of the daisies was the stem of knotgrass which I threw away yesterday morning. It had been retrieved from the courtyard and brought to our room. Can you think who might have put them there?"

The anger drained from Janet's face and she frowned. "Who would want to do a thing like that? The daisies on their own, I suppose, could have been placed there by one of the girls to brighten the room, but in that case, surely, they should have been put in water. And why the knotgrass? It makes no sense. What did Master Underdown have to say about it?"

"He didn't see them, and I decided to say nothing of them until the morning. I brushed them down between the side of the chest and the wall and then forgot them."

There was nothing else I could tell her without giving away the events of the night and my prior knowledge of the murder. I disliked deceiving her, but felt that even her partiality for me could be severely tested if she knew the truth.

She said: "Perhaps you'd better show me. I shall have to visit your chamber sometime this morning to see that all is tidy, so we may as well go now. Wait. I'll tell one of the girls to follow us in a few minutes to sweep the floor and make the beds." She retraced her steps to the kitchen and disappeared briefly inside. When she returned, we made our way together through the great chamber and up the stairs to the room which I had shared with Philip.

Mistress Overy moved ahead of me to open the door, then let out a cry of distress. I peered over her shoulder. The room was in total disarray. Both mattresses and pillows had been ripped open with a knife, and straw and feathers were mixed with yesterday's rushes on the floor. The lid of the cedarwood chest had been left open, propped against the wall, when it had been discovered that there was nothing inside. The contents of my bundle and Philip's saddle-bag were strewn across the room, and the window and its shutter swung wide on their hinges. With dismay, I remembered opening both earlier that morning in order to examine the cudgel more closely for any remaining traces of blood, and I had failed to close either before leaving the room. Yet again, I cursed myself silently for my foolishness, my only excuse being my inexperience in such devious matters.

"But how could anyone have got in?" Mistress Overy demanded.

"Whoever it was climbed up the vine and escaped the same way, exactly as Master Underdown did last night."

She turned to look at me with a sudden, sharp intake of breath. "Of course," she said. "In all the flurry, no one's thought . . . He couldn't have got out through the court-yard. The main gate and the postern were locked. None of us has seen fit to inquire . . . I truly believe our wits have gone wool-gathering.''

I shook my head. ''You've all had other things to think about since the body was discovered, and those sort of questions are for the Sergeant to ask when he gets here.'' I glanced around me. ''Anyway, there's no harm done. Our would-be thief has not found what he came for.''

Janet gave me a curious glance, but forbore to comment. She respected the confidence I had reposed in her, and her silence intimated more plainly than words could have done that she considered my affairs none of her business. But after a moment, she remarked: ''All the same. Master Steward will have to be informed that there has been an intruder in the house. It may have some relevance to the murder.'' She hesitated, then asked: ''How much does Silas Bywater know of you and Master Underdown?''

''He has, as yet, no idea of the truth. He assumes Philip and I were partners, that I have replaced his dead brother, and that we are here as traders, scouring this part of Cornwall for things to buy cheaply and sell overseas at a profit. Including deformed and stunted children.''

A spasm crossed the housekeeper's face, as well it might, at the thought of such revolting traffic, before she returned to the matter in hand. ''I'll go and look for Alwyn,'' she said, ''and tell him what has happened. You proceed as you intended, lad, with your inquiries.''

''Before I go, let me show you what we came to find.'' I closed the lid of the chest, shifted it an inch or two away from the wall, stooped and stood upright again, the bunch of withered flowers in my hand. ''Here! The stem of knotgrass is among the daisies. You see how dry and broken it is? It's the same one, I'm sure, that Silas Bywater gave me at Buckfast on Friday.''

Janet Overy took the tattered nosegay from me and stared at it in bewilderment. Then she shook her head slowly. "It could not have been Silas," she said at last. "He didn't arrive until this morning—unless he entered the chamber the same way Master Underdown left it, and that, I think, is unlikely." She raised her eyes and added shrewdly: "You must have been sleeping soundly not to hear the opening of a window and shutter and the noise of a man heaving himself through to find a foothold on that vine. And if that failed to wake you, I should have thought the cold night air blowing on your face must have roused you long before morning's light. And what did you think when you finally woke to discover Master Underdown's bed empty and the window and shutter set wide?"

Her kindly, still handsome face expressed concern, and I had the feeling that my story of the night's events suddenly appeared to her to be full of holes, now that the first shock of the murder had worn off and she was able to bring her reason to bear on the matter. I also gained the impression that she was trying to put me on my guard; to warn me that these were the sort of questions the Sheriff's officer might ask. For a moment I was tempted to unburden myself to her yet again, to tell her exactly what had happened. But I decided against it. It would be unfair to enmesh her in my lies and so, perhaps, provoke her into untruths of her own in order to protect me. No, far better for me to pursue my course of trying to unmask the real murderer.

I had three main suspects: Silas Bywater, Edgar Warden and the stranger who had stayed the night at the Trenowth inn, and it was the latter who, until now, I had thought the one most likely to elude me. Indeed, I had secretly been afraid that the unknown traveller might have already quit the district, but the ransacking of Philip's and my bedchamber gave me renewed heart that he was still in the neighbourhood. Moreover, a moment's reflection persuaded me that the man, whoever he might be, was not a Woodville agent, but a Lancastrian working for the Tudors.

According to my lord of Gloucester, the Queen's kinfolk only wished Philip dead in case the Duke of Clarence had made him privy to some secret which could be made known to their discredit; in which case, Philip's murder was an end in itself. But for adherents of the House of Lancaster, the finding and destruction of the letter was of nearly equal importance. While they might hope that the death of the royal messenger would prevent its delivery to Duke Francis, they could not be certain of that fact, particularly when it had been discovered that Philip was provided with a companion. For the first time, it occurred to me that I myself could be in some danger.

"You look worried, lad." The housekeeper's voice made me jump: I had for a moment forgotten her presence. She drew close to me, and, echoing my thoughts, said: "And so you might well be if you are determined to go ahead with this scheme of yours. A person who has killed once may have no qualms about doing it a second time if you get in the way. Take my advice and leave questions to the Sergeant from Launceston Castle."

"I can't," I replied reluctantly. "And in answer to your earlier query, I am a very heavy sleeper." It was not true. I still, after almost three years, woke more often than not in the middle of the night and in the early morning for the offices of Matins and Prime. The old disciplines of my novitiate continued to exert their power.

Janet Overy sighed. "Ah well, if that's the case there's no more to be said. But look after yourself. Try not to get into trouble. Now, it's time we were both about our business, I to find Master Steward and you to the village to begin your inquiries. All the same, I wish you'd let well alone."

* * *

As I have said before, in those days Trenowth village was little more than a cluster of cottages huddled around the parish church and the inn. It may have grown in the half-century between then and now—I have never been back to see—but I doubt it, unless later generations have increased in size. Like most small communities, it was sufficient unto itself and did not welcome strangers.

The inn, which was dignified with no particular name, comprised one large room on the lower floor, with accommodation for the landlord and his wife above, and one spare room for any passing traveller. The outhouses included a privy, a hen-coop and a byre for the cow. The ale was brewed in the brewhouse set back among the trees, which also supplied Sir Peveril, his lady and servants up at the manor. The two wenches who waited on the evening revellers slept at home. For all of which information I was indebted to Janet Overy, before I left the house. It would have taken much longer to discover it for myself.

My reception by the landlord was cool, as befitted an unfamiliar face. When I entered, he was just broaching a new keg of ale and he glanced round in annoyance at being disturbed.

"Who are you?" he demanded sourly.

"I'm staying at the manor house. My master was murdered last night. His body was found earlier this morning by the sawyer."

The inn-keeper straightened his back and stared at me. He was an undersized man, but compactly made, giving an impression of strength, something he would need in the business of humping casks and barrels. His colouring was that of the Celt, black hair and blue eyes, and I guessed him to be younger than he looked. A life of small rewards and little comfort had taken its toll and seamed his face with worry.

"So that's who you are. I heard there were two of you.

So what do you want with me? You don't have the air of a man who's come to sup ale."

"I'll have a cup, nevertheless," I said, seating myself on one of the benches ranged along each wall and reaching into my purse for the necessary coins. "After that, perhaps you'd answer me some questions."

"Depends what they are." He plucked a wooden beaker down from a shelf and proceeded to fill it from the newly opened barrel. He added shrewdly: "Not my place to answer anything you might ask. If I did know something of the killing—which I don't!—only the Sheriff's man has a right to hear it."

"True," I acknowledged as I pledged his health. "Nor," I went on handsomely, "would I ask for information about your friends here, in the village. No, my inquiries concern a man who, according to Father Anselm, slept at his inn last night and arrived in Trenowth sometime yesterday morning. He was served all his meals in his room and did not go to Vespers, a fact which seems to have upset the good father."

"Oh, him!" The landlord's manner thawed a little, although even now it could hardly be deemed friendly. "He's gone. Went at first light. Paid his shot and had his horse saddled just on sun-up. Said he had a long day's journey ahead of him."

"Did he say where he was going?" I asked. "This is an excellent ale. Some of the best I've tasted."

A faint glimmer of gratification appeared in the landlord's eyes, but there was no accompanying smile. "He said he had business in Launceston, but whether that's true or not, I'm in no position to hazard. As far as I'm concerned, that's where he went when he left here. Why? What's your interest in him?"

I countered with yet another question. "What was his name? Did he tell you?"

"He said it was Jeremiah Fletcher. And so it may have been, for all that I know."

"What did he look like?" I persisted, but I could see that I was stretching my informant's patience to its limit.

"Polite and quiet and minded his own business, unlike some people I could mention." The landlord relented a trifle and added: "A long, thin face. Sad-looking. A gentleman, well-dressed. Shy, my woman thought him."

I sat staring thoughtfully ahead of me, my ale momentarily forgotten. For, unless I was very much mistaken, I had just been given a description of the gentleman of Buckfast Abbey.

CHAPTER
14

The landlord's voice cut into my reverie. "You know this man?"

"I—er—Yes, I think I may have seen him once before." I asked for another cup of ale, and while it was being drawn, inquired: "Would it be possible . . . ? Could a man leave the inn at night without disturbing you and your good lady?"

He gave a short bark of laughter at this description of his wife and snorted: "Lady, God help us!" under his breath. Still grinning sourly, he placed the refilled mazer in front of me before answering my question. "It's possible, aye, if a man were so foolish as to quit his warm bed to go wandering in the woods." His thin face sharpened with sudden understanding. "Oho, that's the way of it, is it? You think our fine gentleman might be the murderer." The landlord shrugged disparagingly. "He could be, who's to say otherwise? Any man's capable of killing I suppose, although for my money, some are less likely to than others. And this one looked as if he couldn't say boo to a goose."

I didn't argue the point that sheep's clothing can often disguise a wolfish soul, but I did ask, when I had finished and paid for my second cup of ale, if I might look around upstairs.

The landlord gave grudging assent. "But do it quickly, before my wife gets back from her sister's, which she might well do at any time. The stairs are at the side of the house, as you no doubt noticed when you came in. You have to pass through our bedchamber to reach the guest-room."

That information discouraged me for a moment, until I reflected that the landlord and his goodwife probably slept so soundly, worn out by the toils of the day, that very little would disturb their slumbers; certainly not someone in stockinged feet, taking every care not to wake them. So I thanked him and, going outside, mounted the staircase to the upper storey. A door at the top, set in the wall to the left of the tiny landing, opened directly into the chaos of the first bedchamber, where, although the morning was well advanced, the bed was still unmade, the chamber-pot still unemptied, the rushes old and stale-smelling and a rush-light left carelessly burning. I snuffed the flame be-tween my fingers, trusting that all would be put to rights before some other traveller wanted to spend a night at the inn.

I opened the door to the second bedchamber and found that although the bed had been decently covered with a patterned spread dyed blue and green, the room itself smelled no more savoury than the first. The rushes on the floor were, by my reckoning, several days old, and even though there were candles instead of a rush-light, these were made of tallow rather than wax. The "all-night" was untouched, and upon closer inspection I discovered why. The bread was stale and unappetizing and a spider had drowned in the jug of ale.

I returned to the little landing at the top of the stairs and leaned against the wall, drawing in great gulps of fresh air. The scent of river-water, grasses and the faint, distant smell of pine filled my grateful nostrils and cleared my head. I considered the description given to me by the landlord of his last night's visitor, and pictured the man I had met four days ago at Buckfast Abbey. I was sure that they were one and the same. But if this Jeremiah Fletcher were indeed what he seemed to be, refined and rather particular in his ways, would he have chosen to stay at Trenowth? According to Father Anselm, he had arrived yesterday morning with plenty of time, having inspected the accommodation, to ride on towards Launceston . . .

To have *reached* Launceston, and that well before eventide! Surely no one would stop at the Trenowth inn unless circumstances forced his hand, and certainly not when within a day's journey of his goal. No! Jeremiah Fletcher's destination had been Trenowth itself, with what objective I could imagine only too well. And yet, even as common sense told me that I need look no further for Philip's killer, doubts assailed me. The murder had been too clumsy to be the work of a trained assassin, who would hardly have confronted his victim, thus giving warning of his intention and offering a chance, however slender, of self-defence. Philip would have been taken in ambush and stabbed from behind.

I slowly descended the stairs and walked down to the river bank to think. I seated myself on a boulder at the Tamar's edge and listened to the water gently lapping over the stones, one of the most restful sounds in the world. There were few flowers about at that time of year, but the smooth broad leaves of marsh marigold showed in dark shiny patches among the grasses, and the thin spidery stems of lady's smock waved at their reflections in the river. I put my elbows on my knees and rested my chin in my cupped hands, trying to sort out my ideas. Supposing I was wrong, and Jeremiah Fletcher—if that were indeed his name—had murdered Philip, by what means was he able to lure him from the house in the middle of the night? Philip was no fool and had been, moreover, aware of his peril at the hands of someone who wished to take his life. No message, however cunningly phrased, would have persuaded him to such an act of folly. Philip had gone of his own free will to the assignation which had led to his death.

It seemed to me that as far as Jeremiah Fletcher was concerned, I had a number of choices. Firstly, he and the gentleman of Buckfast Abbey were two different people, but that, I felt, was unlikely. The landlord's description of his guest fitted too well with my own recollections. Secondly, he was the same man, but an innocent traveller going about his lawful pursuits. He had finished his business in Tavistock, where he had informed me he was bound, and ridden on towards Launceston. But Tavistock, by my reckoning, lay a good few miles north of Trenowth on the other side of the Tamar. To get here would have sent him back on his tracks and brought him well out of his way. It made no sense and I therefore dismissed the notion. My third choice, having established his intention to kill Philip, was that Jeremiah Fletcher had gone out last night with no other end in view than to reconnoitre the ground, but had fortuitously stumbled upon his quarry waiting for another person. The unexpectedness of the encounter would account for the clumsy killing which had necessitated the employment of both knife and cudgel. And my last choice was that Jeremiah Fletcher had been a secret witness to Philip's murder at hands other than his own. He had then left the inn at first light this morning, but stayed in the vicinity to ransack my room.

I rose to my feet and went back to the inn. The landlord

was fortunately still alone, sweeping the ale-room floor. He looked none too pleased to see me again.

"What now?" he demanded peevishly.

"Two things, if you will. Did this Jeremiah Fletcher say where he had come from or how long he would be staying?"

The landlord shook his head. "Fraid I can't help you there," he said with satisfaction. But as I turned to go with a civil word of thanks for all his trouble, he relented. "He did mention he'd spent the previous night as a guest of the Canons at St. Germans."

Another lie, I thought. I was certain by now that Philip and I had been followed to and from Plymouth in spite of all the care we had taken. That shadow I had seen on the cliff-top, while waiting on the Cornish side of the ferry, had been no trick of my imagination after all. And only a short time after Philip and I had arrived at Trenowth Manor, Jeremiah Fletcher had presented himself at the inn. It made good sense and also convinced me that the two previous attempts on Philip's life had been the work of our assassin. But although the will had been there, I was still not sure that in the end Jeremiah Fletcher had actually done the deed.

The sun was riding towards its zenith by the time I returned to the house for dinner. My stomach had long since told me it was time to eat, and the delicious smells wafting out of the kitchen almost made me drool with hunger. When I entered, Janet Overy and Alwyn the steward were already presiding over a full table, round which were gathered Isobel and Edgar Warden as well as Silas Bywater and the rest of the servants. No one's desire for food seemed to have been affected by the day's tragedy, and if I had hoped to detect any signs of guilt by loss of appetite I was doomed to disappointment.

"You're late, lad," the housekeeper chided as I took my place next to Silas. "But I've kept your dinner hot for you over the brazier." She addressed one of the kitchen-maids at the lower end of the table. "Get Master Chapman his food and look sharp about it!"

The girl hurried to fetch my dinner of rabbit, roasted over the fire with onions and peppercorns and flavoured with thyme and rosemary. For several minutes I could attend to nothing and nobody until I had assuaged the pangs of hunger. By the time I was once more aware of what was going on around me, I had nearly emptied my plate.

"Where have you been all morning?" Silas Bywater hissed in my ear. "You know they won't let us leave here until the Sheriff's officer has been? Not without setting the hue and cry after us, at any rate."

I swallowed the last spoonful of rabbit and looked round at him curiously. "Why? Do you want to?"

"Of course I do," he snapped. "And so would you if you'd any sense. No one wants to be mixed up with the law. Besides, there may be work waiting for me. If there's to be an invasion of St. Michael's Mount, ship's masters will be needed."

"You should have thought of that before you came after us," I replied unfeelingly and turned away from him to smile at the kitchen-maid who had collected my empty dish.

A plate of pastry coffins, filled with apple and cinnamon, had been placed on the table, and the smaller of the housekeeper's young helpers had reappeared from the buttery staggering under the weight of two large pitchers of ale. For a short time silence reigned once more, as we again applied ourselves to the serious business of eating and drinking, but then the steward tapped the table-top for our attention.

"Now we are all gathered together," he said, "I wish to say a few words about the terrible events of this morning. First and foremost, Master Underdown, a friend of Sir Peveril and a guest beneath his roof, has been foully done to death. Secondly, someone has ransacked his room, although I gather—" and here he glanced at me "—that nothing was stolen." There was a general murmuring at this, as though most of those present had, until this moment, been ignorant of the fact. "Therefore," the steward went on, "I trust that every one of us will tell the Sergeant, when he arrives from Launceston, whatever he or she knows."

"Well, I know nothing and neither does Isobel, so there's nothing to tell." Edgar Warden's tone was aggressive and he glared round the table as though daring us to contradict him. "We were together all night, as husband and wife should be, and we never left the compound. How could we, when the gates were locked?"

The laundress frowned. "How did Master Underdown get out?"

"He climbed down the vine outside our bedchamber window," I answered. "But surely there are other ways of getting in and out of the house at night, if only you know them?"

But all those who lived in the house and were not village people strenuously denied this. I was a little disconcerted until it dawned on me that, in spite of Alwyn's exhortation they would stand together, preferring to believe, indeed persuading themselves, that the crime was the work of an outsider.

"Whatever your master was doing skulking about the woods at dead of night," Edgar continued truculently, "it had nothing to do with anyone here."

"Nor with anyone down in the village," the baker added.

I glanced at Janet Overy for support, but she merely smiled and said: "Leave it to the Sheriff's officer, lad, that's my advice. He'll know the proper questions to ask."

But later, when the others had returned to work or quit the kitchen, and the pots and dishes had been washed and left to dry on the wide stone ledge beneath one of the open windows, she linked her arm through mine and said: "Come to my room and tell me what happened this morning."

I followed her out of the kitchen to the servants' quarters. The weather had changed yet again, the clouds blowing away inland and a little thin sunshine giving a faint warmth to the sheltered courtyard. Silas was sitting on a bench, his back resting against the wall, talking desultorily to the groom, who was eating a hunk of bread and a slab of goat's milk cheese. I wondered aloud why he had not joined the rest of us for dinner. Janet Overy laughed and said it was because Isobel Warden had objected to his presence at meals, saying that he smelled too much of horses.

"And a woman only has to look as she does and you fools of men will leap to do her bidding," Janet added scornfully.

We went under an archway into a flagged passage and then into a room on the left, with a small horn-paned window, now open to let in light and air from the courtyard. A narrow bed took up most of one wall and a clothes-chest another, with a brazier for winter warmth in a corner and a chair with carved arms drawn close to it. A bag containing flint and tinder hung from a nail near the window embrasure, on which stood a wooden candlestick and candle. There was also a low stool for resting the feet on, but which I now drew close to the armchair and, folding my long legs as best I might, lowered myself on to it, not without a certain amount of discomfort.

"You shouldn't have grown so tall," Janet laughed, seating herself and looking down at me. "So! What did you discover at the inn?"

I recounted faithfully all that had happened. Although she was much too young and was still a handsome woman, talking to her was a little like talking to my mother; I felt the same sense of comfort in her presence as I had experienced in the long-gone days when my mother was alive and I sat at her knee confiding my day's adventures. And when I had finished, I waited with the same desire for approbation.

There was silence for a moment or two, then she said with a deep sigh of what sounded like relief: "I think there can be no doubt that you have uncovered the murderer. If you tell all to the Sheriff's officer when he arrives this evening as you have told it to me, with the same frankness and giving him the same benefit of your reasoning, I am sure he will be satisfied and set about finding this Jeremiah Fletcher."

I was somewhat disappointed that she had not followed my arguments through to the end. "But I am not certain that he is the murderer. I am certain that the intent was there, and that he had already made two attempts on Master Underdown's life, but as I explained, I cannot wholly reconcile myself to the belief that, in the end, his was the hand that wielded the knife and bludgeon."

She laughed softly at that and shook her head. "And I think you want to make a mystery where none exists. You are young. You crave excitement. Take the word of someone older and wiser than yourself, you have the answer to what has happened."

"But Philip would never have gone to meet Master

Fletcher, even if Master Fletcher had managed to get a message to him without my knowledge."

"Oh no! I think your guess that he had a secret tryst with Isobel Warden is the right one. That could easily have been made yesterday morning while you were out and he was supposed to be sleeping."

I sat up straighter on the stool and linked my hands around my knees. The afternoon was growing yet fairer and sunlight spread across the broad stone sill. "But how would she have got out to meet him? At dinner, you all said that no one could leave the compound after the gates were locked at night."

"Dear lad, use your common sense. There are other windows on this lower storey. Locking the gates may keep intruders out, but it cannot stop anyone unbarring the shutters from within."

"No, I suppose not," I answered slowly. "I should have thought of that. But why then do you suppose Master Underdown took the risk of climbing down the vine?"

She shrugged. "Because he thought it preferable perhaps to roaming a strange house in the dark. Because he was afraid of rousing you when he rose and dressed and left the room, but by putting you to sleep outside the door he was able to leave without any such fear by the window. Because it made him feel young and gallant and adventurous. Who can tell? It might have been any or all of those reasons."

I slewed round on the stool to face her directly. "Do you think, then, that Mistress Warden may have witnessed the murder?"

Janet had plainly not thought of this before, but now gave it her fullest consideration. "It is possible," she admitted at last, "but if you have any kindness towards her, forbear to question her. If she indeed kept the tryst and was witness to the killing, it will have been punishment enough. Do nothing, I beg of you, nothing at all to arouse her husband's suspicions. Edgar is a very jealous man who still cannot quite believe his luck in catching such a prize. And he has reason, for the girl, I think, has begun to regret her marriage and to wish that she had waited a little longer before making her choice. She has a roving eye, that's for sure, and is likely to have been flattered rather than offended by Master Underdown's advances. If he had asked her to meet him last night, it's doubtful if she would have said him nay.''

CHAPTER

15

 There was another, more protracted silence between us while I pondered her words. Then I
said: "If what you think is true, is it not possible
that her husband woke and discovered her absence? If he had gone in search of her and found the open
window, would he not have followed and maybe come
across Isobel and Philip? In that case, could he not be the
murderer?"

Janet Overy rose abruptly to her feet, striking her hands
together in exasperation. "Why do you insist on making
everything more complex than it need be? You are convinced, and have convinced me, that there was a man in the
village last night who has twice made an attempt on Master
Underdown's life. Why look further? Or if you must, why
not glance in Silas Bywater's direction, since on his own
admission he was in the neighbourhood at the time of the
killing, and a sworn enemy of Underdown." She paced
angrily around the little room, beating her clenched fists
against her snowy apron, to that the bunch of keys at her

waist jumped and rattled. "Not that I believe him any more guilty of the crime than Edgar. You have told me that the Duke of Gloucester hired you for the very purpose of guarding his agent from attack. His Grace was expecting just such an occurrence, and he was right to do so. You and Master Underdown were followed from Exeter—to Buckfast, to Plymouth and now here. So why, therefore, do you insist on looking for guilt elsewhere?"

Sympathy welled up in me for this woman who had already had so much misfortune in her life. She had at last found a pleasant home, a haven from the storms which had tossed her, a place where she was valued and could be of use. Now death had once again come calling, and violent death at that, to disrupt her quiet existence; but at least it need not tear her safe little world apart if the murder was proved to be the work of an outsider. I was tempted to let the matter lie. She was right: I had enough evidence, along with Philip's tokens of credence from the King, to convince the Sheriff's officer that the murder was the work of a political assassin, and that he need do no more than send a letter to Westminster. I had no doubt that King Edward's own agents would hunt down and deal with Jeremiah Fletcher. It would be a satisfactory ending to an unsavoury affair.

And yet . . . I was irked by the thought that Philip's real murderer might go free, even though I should shed no tears for Jeremiah Fletcher. Janet saw my hesitation and gripped both my hands in hers.

"Promise me, Roger, that you'll pursue your inquiries no further."

I found myself in a dilemma. I liked and was sorry for her. I wanted desperately to do as she asked, but my desire to discover the truth was greater. If it turned out that her reading of the solution was correct, no one would be better pleased than I; but until that was certain, I was loath to let the matter rest. "Nosiness," my mother had called it when I was young; a desire to stick that member into other people's business. John Selwood, the Abbot of Glastonbury, had been kinder and, when sanctioning my release from the Order, had referred to my "insatiable curiosity," piously hoping that I would always use it in the quest for truth.

I sent up a small prayer for guidance which was immediately answered, or so it seemed to me, by a rap on the door and the appearance a moment later of Father Anselm. Janet Overy dropped my hands and turned to welcome him with her ready smile. I rose to my feet, relieved that I had made no promise, and edged towards the open doorway, ready to make my escape.

"Wait, my son!" The priest detained me with a hand on my sleeve. "You will no doubt wish to hear what I have to say. A traveller from Plymouth, passing through the village not half an hour since, informed me that news was cried in the city early this morning that the King has sent orders for Sir Henry Bodrugan and the Sheriff of Cornwall to levy the *posse comitatus* and reduce St. Michael's Mount as soon as possible. The messenger who carried the orders was already across the Tamar and on his way to Sir John at Truro, where he should be by tomorrow morning at the latest, travelling as he was with the greatest speed and urgency. So now all we can do is wait for further news and pray for their success."

My first thought was to wonder what instructions had been sent to the Master of the *Falcon*. Was his ship to be part of the assault on the Mount or would he be ordered to Plymouth to pick up Philip? Either way, I must return to the city as soon as I could. Today, St. Faith's Day, was Tuesday and he had promised to be back at the Turk's Head by the end of the week. But the messengers who had set out for London last Thursday, as soon as Oxford's invasion was known, had made better time than anyone had expected, given the state of most of the roads. And the King had wasted no time either in sending them back again with his orders. It behoved me, therefore, to leave Trenowth as soon as possible; tomorrow for preference, once I had settled matters with the Sheriff's officer. Which was yet another reason to accept Janet's wisdom, and what, deep down, I more than half believed myself: that I had found the answer to Philip's murder.

Father Anselm's voice cut across my thoughts. He was speaking now of the terrible event which had brought him to the manor house, expressing his condolences to me on the death of my master. I did my best to look as a bereaved servant should.

"Fortunate indeed," the priest continued, "that he made his confession only last night and received absolution. There can be no question as to his state of grace. I understand the Sergeant has been sent for from Launceston Castle and that you must await his coming. But after that, what plans do you have, my son, for the removal or burial of the body?"

Such considerations had not yet crossed my mind, and I realized with a shock that I would be looked to as the proper person to make these dispositions. I realized also that I knew nothing about Philip except that his brother was dead. He had mentioned no other family, but for aught I could tell he might have a wife and children, parents perhaps, somewhere in his native city of Bristol. But a body could not remain unburied for any length of time, not even when sealed in its coffin, and I had other things to do which would take me across the sea for several weeks.

"If you will conduct his funeral and bury him in the churchyard here, Father," I said firmly, "that will be best." And a better resting-place than you deserve, Master Underdown, I thought grimly, here, by the banks of this lovely river, among the lush Cornish grass and within smell of the distant sea. "He lies now in the great hall," I added. "The door is locked, but Master Steward has the key. I'm sure Mistress Overy will fetch it for you if you wish to view the body."

Janet could do no other than comply and reluctantly conducted the priest in search of Alwyn, but she gave me an imploring, backward glance across her shoulder. Leave well alone, it said, you have your answer. This is my home, and you and Philip Underdown have already brought it trouble enough.

I followed Mistress Overy and Father Anselm from the housekeeper's room, but not into the courtyard. Instead I turned back along the flagged passageway, thoughtfully considering the other doors set in the walls on either side of it. One gave access to the room of Edgar and Isobel Warden, but I had no means of knowing which. There was no alternative but to knock on each one in turn and trust that Isobel herself would answer my summons. She had disappeared from the kitchen after dinner directly the meal was finished, not offering to help with the dishes. There had been no sign of her in the courtyard earlier, and I thought it unlikely, in the circumstances, that she would have gone walking in the woods alone. I could only hope that she had retired to her room.

I was in luck. I knocked on the first two doors I came to without evoking any response, but after waiting a moment outside the third, I heard a rustling noise within the room. Seconds later the door opened to reveal Isobel Warden, slightly dishevelled but looking more beautiful than ever, her red hair unbraided and cascading over her shoulders as far as her knees. The green eyes were clouded, unfocused, and the untidy bed, visible in the background, indicated that she had been asleep. This did not surprise me; all her movements were languorous and I suspected that there was only one pleasure that would keep her awake for any length of time.

"You!" she exclaimed, astonished, but not displeased. Her eyes, now alert and wide open, raked me slowly from head to foot. She held the door wider. "Come in and sit down."

The room which I entered was of much the same proportions and furnished in the same way as the housekeeper's, but there the likeness ended. Janet Overy's room was as neat and as shining as a new pin, while this was untidy enough to remind me forcibly of the Trenowth inn. Clothes spilled from the chest or were tossed, unfolded, on the floor and chair and window-sill. The smell of unwashed linen was overlaid with the musty scent of perfumed oils and unguents, which came from a collection of unstoppered phials and small pots on a shelf above the bed. The bed itself was covered with a piece of rich red silk, probably from the east and purchased from some passing chapman. I often carried such rolls of material myself, obtained directly from trading-ships docked in the ports of Southampton, London or Bristol. But this was stained with patches of candle grease and other marks, less identifiable. Whatever talents Isobel Warden possessed, housewifery was not among them.

She waved me to a stool and herself curled up on the bed, propped on one elbow. A languid smile curled the red lips as she asked the question she should have put earlier. "What do you want?"

I regarded her curiously while considering how best to reply. She did not look at all like someone who had witnessed a brutal murder only some twelve hours before. Surely even a person as heartless as she appeared to be would have been marked by such an experience. There would have been some lurking horror at the back of the eyes, some expression of regret or terror. But her glance held nothing but invitation, which I did my best to ignore.

I passed my tongue over lips which were suddenly dry and cast about in my mind for the necessary words. "Master Underdown," I said at last. "You liked him?"

Her eyes widened almost, I could have sworn, with indignation. This was not what she had expected. Then she shrugged. "I've seen worse men," she admitted. "But he was old. He could have been the same age as my father."

I had to suppress a smile at the thought of Philip's outrage had he been able to hear her. But my mirth did not last long.

"He was a fine figure of a man, nevertheless," I pressed her.

"I've already said, I've seen worse."

"Did . . . did he attract you?"

She frowned, seemingly still ignorant of the path along which I was leading her. "I hardly saw him, only at breakfast and at dinner yesterday. A forward man with a bold eye, but I'm used to that. It doesn't disturb me."

"Nor the fact that he put his arm about your waist? Nor that your husband was angry?"

Her face clouded at this; a sullen expression which spoke of contempt, but also of fear. Nothing could have told me more plainly that she disliked Edgar and that Janet Overy was right: she was beginning to regret a marriage into which, no doubt, her parents and her own ambition had pushed her, for as bailiff to Sir Peveril Trenowth, Edgar's standing in the community was greater than hers.

"My husband is always angry if another man so much as looks at me." She shrugged and gave me an upward glance beneath her long, thick lashes. "I don't know what he'd do if he found you here, a strong, handsome lad like you. Oh, don't fret! He won't return until supper-time."

She stretched herself full-length on the bed, linking her hands behind her head, the upthrust of her breasts beneath the dark green woollen gown full and inviting. She had removed her shoes, and now wriggled her bare toes provocatively. I felt suddenly hot and embarrassed.

It was two years since, at the age when many men are already fathers, I had laid my first girl in the long, lush grasses which border the River Stour, and from then on I had hardly lived like the monk my mother had wished me to be. There had been girls at fairs, where I had gone to sell my wares, in villages through which I had passed, in towns and cities, and all of them willing and knowledgeable. (I would never force myself on any woman or deflower the innocent.) But there was something about Isobel Warden which made me uncomfortable. She was certainly beautiful, one of the loveliest girls I had ever seen, and with the promise of an even richer beauty as she grew older. But for some reason, it was that which made me uneasy. Had she been less stridently female I might have been attracted to her, but such blatant femininity I found unnerving. Philip, on the other hand, would not have done so, and I decided that there was nothing for it but to put my question bluntly, and to hope that its abruptness shocked her into telling me the truth.

"Did you and Master Underdown have a tryst last night in the woods?"

I don't know what reaction I had expected; self-righteous denial, the furious indignation of guilt, perhaps. What I had not been prepared for was the look of frank amazement which she turned on me, followed by the snapping together of her brows in bewildered curiosity.

"Why do you think that?" she asked me.

"He obviously fell victim to your charms when he saw you at breakfast yesterday, nor did I think you adverse to him. He was a man who took what he wanted, and there was no doubt in my mind that he wanted you."

Isobel gave me a small, superior smile, as one who knew men.

"Not enough to risk another beating from my husband. Master Underdown had sufficient sense to recognize that he was no match for Edgar. Edgar is young, and in a fight that will always give the more youthful participant the edge. And in my life I have met one or two men like your master; men who hold such high opinions of themselves that they consider no woman worth imperilling their precious skins for."

I sat staring at her, chewing my underlip, which is a habit I have when perplexed, as my children are never tired of pointing out to me. I found myself believing her against my will. For one thing, she neither looked nor behaved like a young woman who had witnessed murder done, or who had even stumbled, later, across the body. For another, there was truth in what she said about Philip's character: I could well imagine that he would not have thought any woman worth the risk of humiliation or pain. I accepted his boast that he had had practise enough with jealous husbands, but that was in the past when he was younger and could outwit or outfight them. And yet . . .

"He could have wished for revenge," I said. "Your husband felled him with a single blow, and called down upon his head a rebuke from Master Steward. My . . . my master would have found that hard to forgive."

Again she shrugged, the red lips pulled down at the corners. "That may be, and no doubt, had he lived, he would have taken his revenge in one way or another. A letter of complaint to Sir Peveril or a word in the ear of someone with influence to get Edgar dismissed from his office. But not the risk of seducing his wife. Besides," she added, anger suddenly informing her voice, "what makes you so sure that I would have been party to a tryst, supposing he had proposed it?''

"Would you not?'' I asked directly.

"No.'' Her green eyes, wide and innocent, bereft of all coquetry, met mine in a candid stare. "He was well-looking enough, I grant you. A handsome man in his time. But there was something about him which I did not like.'' She gave a slight shiver. "Something which repelled me.''

She spoke with such sincerity that I was left with very little choice but to believe her. And I understood what she meant about Philip. I, too, had experienced that feeling of repulsion. It was as though he had had some deformity, not of the body but of the soul.

I rubbed a hand across my eyes. "Do you swear,'' I asked at length, "that you did not meet Master Underdown on the river bank last night? That your husband did not follow? That there was no fight between them which resulted in Master Underdown's death?''

Her eyebrows rose again at this. "So that's what you were thinking? That Edgar did murder because he was jealous?'' She pulled herself into a sitting position and swung her legs off the bed so that she was facing me once more. She leaned forward and placed both her hands in mine. "I swear to you, by God's Holy Mother, that Master Underdown neither asked me, nor did I accept such a proposal.'' Then she slid off the bed, bent her head and planted a kiss full on my lips.

I dropped her hands, sprang to my feet and withdrew hurriedly to the other side of the room. I could tell by the look on her face that she was unused to having her advances treated like this. In her own way, she was every bit as vain as Philip.

"I must go,'' I said, edging towards the door. The room suddenly felt close and fetid; I could not escape quickly enough.

The door swung inwards and Edgar Warden stood on the threshold, his right hand nursing his left.

"I've driven a nail into my thumb," he grunted at Isobel. "Do you have any of that sicklewort salve left that Janet gave you?" He became aware of my presence and turned with an oath to face me. "What in God's name are you doing here," he demanded, "alone with my wife?"

Isobel was swift to take her revenge for my having spurned her. "He thinks you may be the murderer," she said.

CHAPTER
16

Edgar Warden stared at me, dumbfounded, the wound in his thumb for the moment forgotten. He also blenched, his weatherbeaten skin turning a shade paler than when he had first entered the room.

"Eh?" he spluttered. "What do you mean? Thinks I may be the murderer? What are you talking about, woman?"

Isobel smiled maliciously. "He thinks you found me last night with Master Underdown and killed him in a fit of jealous rage. When you know," she added virtuously, "that I was by your side all through the hours of darkness, as a good wife should be. You woke at least three times and I was always there."

Edgar's eyes became two slits in a face as suddenly red as it had previously been white. He raised two clenched fists the size of small hams and advanced on me threateningly, kicking the door shut behind him.

"He thinks that, does he?" He thrust his congested features close to mine. "I don't mind you calling me a murderer," he said, "because if any man fooled with my wife I would kill him. But I won't have you or anybody else casting doubts on her virtue, and for that, you're going to get the thrashing of your life."

Now, if there was one thing I learned in the art of self-preservation during my years on the road, it was to react swiftly to any threat of violence. If a man said he was going to punch me, I wasted no time wondering if he meant it, but took him at his word and got my blow in first, as I did then. The words were barely out of Edgar's mouth before my right fist caught him squarely on the jaw, making him lose his balance and stumble back against the foot of the bed, and while he was still dazed, I made a craven bid for the door. He was too quick for me, however, catching me round the ankles and bringing me crashing to the floor. Now it was my turn to try to gather my shaken wits, by which time he had lost control of himself and locked his hands around my throat. Although I tried to tear them loose, his grip was too strong and the blood was thundering in my ears.

Isobel screamed, genuinely frightened by the fury she had unleashed, and joined her efforts with mine to get her husband off me. In the end, between us, we succeeded and I staggered to my feet while Isobel tried to calm Edgar, but was pushed roughly away for her trouble. He launched himself at me again, but I managed to step aside so that his fist crashed into the wall behind me. But he was beyond feeling hurt, and I doubt if he was even conscious of the pain until much later. With a snarl of rage he drew back his arm for another attempt, but once more I anticipated his onslaught and sent him sprawling to the floor. And on this occasion I was through the door and heading for the court-yard before he had picked himself up.

"What's happened? What's been going on?" It was Ja-net Overy's voice, sharp with disapproval, as she approached the servants' quarters from the direction of the great hall.

I must have looked the worse for wear, with my hair and clothes awry and my hands tenderly feeling my neck where Edgar had bruised it. And Edgar himself, erupting furiously through the door behind me, showed a rapidly swelling jaw, while several dark red welts disfigured his face. When he saw Janet, however, he reluctantly lowered his hands, but continued to watch me with a malevolence that was in itself like a physical attack.

"It was my fault," I said. "I was making some inquiries of Mistress Warden and Edgar mistook my purpose. He thought I was accusing him of murder."

"And my wife of adultery!" he spat.

"It was a mistake," I said lamely. "I just want to find out who killed Master Underdown, that's all."

"I warned that you would do nothing but harm," the housekeeper reproached me. "Such questions are for the Sheriff's officer if he thinks it needful to ask them. Edgar!" She looked sternly at the bailiff. "Go and get Isobel to patch up your wounds, then return to your duties." She beckoned me. "As for you, follow me and I'll find you some salve for that throat which seems to be giving you so much trouble. Let there be no more of this nonsense!"

Muttering under his breath in a manner that boded me ill, Edgar retraced his steps to his room and his wife's ministrations. Recollecting his pierced thumb, he stuck it in his mouth to suck it, then bit it at me in the time-honoured gesture of contempt and defiance. I pretended not to see and accompanied Janet back to her room where she kept her salves and unguents.

She reached up to a shelf and brought down a small earthenware pot from which she carefully removed the lid.

"Linseed oil and honey," she said, scooping out a spoonful and holding it over the brazier. "Applied warm, it will prevent injuries from swelling. Open the neck of your shirt so I can get at you. Those are some nasty bruises you have there."

"My own fault, you think," I suggested sheepishly, doing as she asked.

She spread a little of the ointment on her fingers and began gently to rub my throat. "Yes," she answered frankly, "but I suppose you felt you had to do it. So, what did you learn from the fair Isobel and her husband?" I winced as she pressed a particularly tender spot, and was glad when she stood back, surveying her handiwork. "That will do for now. You may find difficulty in swallowing for a while, but I doubt Edgar's done you any lasting harm." She reached up once more to the shelf and brought down a small glass bottle from which she tipped a single pill. "Here. These tablets are made from dried lettuce juice. Taken in quantity, they can put you to sleep, but one will relax you and ease the pain. So," she went on, replacing her medicines in their accustomed place, "you haven't yet answered my question."

I laced up the neck of my shirt again and swallowed the pill as I had been bidden. After a moment's consideration, I said: "I think we may have been wrong in assuming it was to meet Isobel that Master Underdown left the house last night. Either she has greater powers of deception than I would credit her with possessing, or I am more gullible than I think I am. But either way, I now believe her innocent, and therefore her husband also. Nevertheless," I added defiantly, "there is still Silas Bywater."

Janet heaved a resigned sigh. "I suppose I can't stop you making trouble there either, even though you have the answer to the riddle under your nose." She laid an affectionate hand on my shoulder. "But tread warily with that one, lad. I've grown fond of you in the short time I've known you. My son should have looked like you, tall and fair and straight, with the same powerful muscles. I wouldn't want any harm to befall you, and I think Silas Bywater an unscrupulous man. So take care. But I'd much rather you believed in your own powers of discernment and accepted that this Jeremiah Fletcher is the killer, and for the very reasons you were set to guard Philip Underdown."

I raised my hand and laid it over hers. "I know what you say makes sense, but . . ." I broke off with a lift of my shoulders.

She withdrew her hand with a sorrowful look. "You must do as you see fit and I can only urge you to think twice about it. But if you need a friend, you know where to find me, either here or in the kitchen or about the house somewhere. Which reminds me," she added in sudden consternation, "the hours are slipping by and it will soon be four o'clock and time for supper. Heaven alone knows what those good-for-nothing girls are doing in my absence." She smoothed down her apron and straightened her hood. "You will find, I hope, that your room has been set to rights, so if you wish to rest for a while, you may."

Once more I followed her from her room just as Edgar Warden emerged from his. I noted that his thumb was bound and that salve adorned the weals on his face. He gave me an evil look, but had evidently promised Isobel that he would make no more trouble because, with a curt nod to Janet Overy, he pushed past us and went on his way across the courtyard, and was lost to view beneath the archway. The housekeeper hurried in the direction of the kitchen, her step quickened by the sound of chatting and giggling within. I smiled to myself. While the cat had been away, the little mice had played, and I would not have wished myself into the shoes of either of the kitchen-maids. Janet's wrath, I suspected, could be formidable.

I glanced around, but Silas Bywater had disappeared. The groom was talking to the carter who had just arrived with fresh bales of hay for the stables, and these were being unloaded by two men whom I guessed to be the James and Luke referred to yesterday by Mistress Overy; village men who took their meals at home and not with the household servants. Judging by the way they gesticulated and their earnest, excited faces, they and John Groom were regaling the carter with news of the murder. How he was reacting to it was difficult to see, for, like all his kind, he wore a large felt hat with a concealing brim to protect him from the elements. I gave them all the time of day as I passed beneath the archway.

I followed the path down through the woods to the village. I needed to be on my own; to try to get my teeming thoughts into some sort of order. But the more they chased one another round inside my head, the more I became convinced that Janet was right and that Jeremiah Fletcher was the murderer. He was a Tudor agent, that House being the one faint hope the Lancastrians now had of regaining power, even though it was through a bastard line which had been barred by King Henry IV from ever ascending the throne of England. But although that fact now seemed fairly settled in my mind, I was still left with the mystery of why Philip had escaped from our room last night. Who was it he had gone to meet, if not Isobel Warden? And the more I went over our talk together, the more certain I felt that she had told me the truth; that the amazement she had shown at my suggestion of a tryst had been genuine; that her reading of Philip's character was sounder than mine.

I turned aside from the path to the river bank, to the spot where, last night, I had knelt beside Philip's body, and where, this morning, the sawyer had found him. The long grasses were still flattened, although beginning here and there to spring upright, and there were dark patches of blood on the ground. I made a methodical search of the surrounding area and, after some minutes, came to the conclusion that Philip had been struck down where he had fallen. There were no signs that I could see of the body having been dragged to its resting-place and no traces of blood elsewhere to indicate that that was where he had been killed. Furthermore, I suspected that if that had happened, Philip would have been turned on to his back, for it is easier in my experience to drag a man face up rather than the other way around.

There were indications that the grass had been trampled by more than one person, but some of the damage could be accounted for by my own tracks, and it was difficult to say whether two or three people had been there before me. If Jeremiah Fletcher were the assassin, then someone else must surely have been present as well, for I held by my conviction that Philip would never have been foolish enough to be lured away from the house by any kind of message without first checking to see if it were false. And the only other person beside Isobel Warden whom he might have crept away to meet was Silas Bywater.

I repaired to the inn, partly to ease my aching throat and partly to consider this theory in comfort. As I had guessed, the ale-room was almost empty at that time in the afternoon, when most people were about their business on the manor. There was only one other man seated on a bench under the window, his thin legs stretched out before him, his head resting against the wall at his back. A mazer of ale, half drunk, stood on the table in front of him, his body was slack, his eyes drowsily closed, although now and then the lids lifted slightly as he cast a glance in my direction. I sat down on the other side of the room and ignored him.

The landlord was nowhere to be seen, but the determined, muscular-looking woman who attended to my needs could only be his wife, and I decided he might have good reason to be wary of her. When she had served me, I too leaned my head back against the wall and closed my eyes, but not to sleep. In my mind's eye I summoned up the image of Silas Bywater and considered him.

If he had indeed sent a message to Philip, when could Philip have received it without my knowledge? The answer was the same as before; yesterday morning after breakfast, when I was out searching for the man Philip was supposed to have seen from the bedchamber window, and when I presumed him to be asleep on his bed. So, having settled that, I came to my second question. Why had Silas summoned him to a secret meeting? Because, as he had hinted to me on more than one occasion, he knew something to Philip's detriment and was intending to threaten him with it in order to get the money he felt was his due. But why had Philip agreed to the assignation? There was, to my mind, and as I had told myself earlier, only one answer. The time, the place, could both have been at Philip's suggestion with one end in view; to rid himself of a man who had suddenly reappeared in his life and who threatened to become an embarrassment. Philip had set out to murder Silas, but had himself been killed instead, either by his intended victim or by Jeremiah Fletcher, who had accidentally discovered them together.

Before I had time to pursue this argument any further, to find out its flaws or lack of them, my thoughts were interrupted by my fellow drinker.

"Here's a to-do, then, for the county. Though it's too far away to worry we, I reckon." I realized that he was referring to the Earl of Oxford's invasion and not the event uppermost in my mind, Philip's murder, which suggested that he was a stranger to the village. I nodded, loath to give him more encouragement, but he went on, undeterred: "The King'll sort it out, no doubt."

"No doubt," I said and closed my eyes again, willing him to do the same.

"'E's a good King, is Edward. Better for the likes o' we than poor old Henry, and 'e's got 'is brothers t'back 'im up. Leastways, 'e's got Duke Richard. Don't know as I reckon much to t'other 'un." Having disposed thus unceremoniously of George of Clarence, he asked: "You from the village?"

Cornered, I opened my eyes and answered grudgingly: "No. Just passing through. I'm lodging for a day or so at the manor house. I have friends there among the servants." This was no lie. I could certainly claim Janet Overy as a friend.

The information seemed to intrigue him. "So you know 'em up there, do you? You'll be missing the fun."

I stared at the man stupidly. "Fun?" I repeated.

He drank off the rest of his ale, then nodded. "Aye. I come up from St. Germans this morning with a load of hay for Sir Peveril Trenowth's stables. I'm a carter by trade," he added. "But a fellow stopped me just short o' the village and offered me this if I'd let 'im take my place for an hour or so." He plunged his hand into the pouch at his belt and proudly produced a gold farthing, as the quarter noble used to be called in those days. "Said 'e was a friend of Alwyn the steward and wanted to play a trick on 'im. Said Alwyn'd bet 'im two angels that 'e couldn't get into the house without 'im knowing." The man put the coin away again and looked at me, a little shamefaced. "Not sure I altogether believed 'im, but I don't get the chance o' many gold coins in my job, an' besides, 'e was well-spoken and well-dressed." It was clear that the carter had allowed his greed to override his better judgement. "A gentleman, you might say, so quite likely 'is story was true after all. 'E's quite likely to be a friend of this Alwyn. 'E borrowed my hat, as well, so's 'e could hide 'is face. 'You want to take off that tunic, too,' I tells 'im. 'No one'll think you're a carter dressed like that.' So 'e did, but I don't think 'e quite trusted me. Took it with 'im, under the bales of fodder.''

I lumbered to my feet, almost overturning the table in my hurry. "A thin-faced man?" I asked. "Narrow features?"

" 'Es. You could say that. A bit weasely maybe, now you come to mention it. But a gentleman, for all that," he insisted defiantly.

"That doesn't make him any the less a rogue," I snapped, yelling for the landlord's wife so that I could pay my shot. "You fool! Do you think there aren't evil men among our betters, just as there are among the lower orders?"

The carter had grown pale and his hand shook as he put his mazer down on the table. "You know this man?" he asked apprehensively.

I nodded, turning to pay the goodwife of the inn, who had arrived breathing fire and slaughter at the imperiousness of my summons. I gave her over the odds to placate her. As I made for the door, I paused to lay my hand reassuringly on the carter's arm.

"Don't worry. You may have done me a service if I can catch this man. I know what he has come for and most probably where to find him. Where did you arrange to meet him to reclaim your wagon? No matter! You had better follow me to the house when you are ready."

And I was through the ale-room door and running up the path before, now thoroughly alarmed, he could question me further.

CHAPTER 17

The rutted track was barred with long October shadows and the pale sunshine struggled to make itself felt between the dying leaves of the overhanging trees. A late-flowering patch of musk mallow, its pale rose blooms nodding at the end of fragile stalks, gleamed corpse-like among the ragged grasses. A bird sang high in the branches above me, and the river rippled on its gentle way somewhere below. So much beauty, but I had eyes and ears for none of it: my thoughts were fixed entirely on Jeremiah Fletcher.

The man had to be desperate to try such a ruse in broad daylight, ready even to brave the possibility of finding me or someone else in my room. He must have felt his luck to be in when he saw me leave the courtyard, and I felt that my luck was in that he had seen me. For now he would be lulled into a sense of false security, believing himself to have time to search the bedchamber again with less chance of being interrupted. He would look more thoroughly than he had done this morning, when he had climbed in through the window and had, perforce, to make his exit the same way. It was a means of ingress and egress he had not dared use in mid-afternoon. I wondered what excuse he had made to gain access to the great chamber and the stairs.

My footsteps sounded hollowly as I raced beneath the archway. At first, I thought the courtyard deserted because the sun was in my eyes. But as my vision cleared, I saw James and Luke and John Groom beside the cart, humping bales of hay on to their shoulders, ready to carry them across to the stables.

"Where is he?" I shouted. "Where's the carter?"

They all gaped at me for a moment, bewildered by my urgency of tone. Then the man who I later learned was James pointed in the direction of the house. 'E wanted to use the privy. I told 'im there was three, an' 'e chose to go indoors. Said 'e'd never seen the inside of a gentleman's house and t'would be a rare opportunity fer 'im to do so."

I was running towards the great chamber door before he had finished speaking, calling over my shoulder: "Come with me quickly! He's no carter! He's a thief!" Out of the corner of my eye, I saw them exchange dubious glances, wondering if I'd taken leave of my senses and debating whether or not they should ignore my commands. "Hurry!" I shouted. "It's true, I swear it!" I paused with my hand on the latch of the great chamber door. "One of you fetch Alwyn and rouse the servants! The other two follow me!"

I could not wait to see if they obeyed, if my voice had contained sufficient authority to impress them, but turned and went inside. I ran across the room and mounted the stairs two at a time, not even bothering to look in the garderobe, so convinced was I that it would be empty. And I was right. As I glanced along the corridor, I could see that the door to my bedchamber stood ajar, and the sound of stealthy movements could be heard from inside.

Checking my headlong rush, I drew in several deep breaths to steady myself before creeping forward to peer through the crack. Then I pushed wide the door.

"You won't find what you're looking for," I said. "It's not there."

The startled face which turned towards me, the wide-brimmed hat now discarded, was unmistakably that of the man from Buckfast Abbey, and undoubtedly that of Jeremiah Fletcher who had stayed last night at the Trenowth inn. He had not, this time, created the havoc of his earlier visit. What was the point? If the letter had not been hidden in the pillows or mattresses before, it was unlikely to be concealed now in their replacements. But everything else which belonged either to Philip or myself, had been gathered into a pile on one of the beds and was being thoroughly searched item by item.

The man had been crouching on the floor, but now he sprang to his feet, his hand groping at his waist for the dagger in his belt, only to realize with dismay that he had put it off, together with his tunic, when he had assumed his disguise of the carter. The recollection brought with it a wave of panic, and for the second time in little more than an hour, I found myself the object of a murderous attack. But now I was truly afraid, for this man was used to killing, and he would not scruple to murder me if he got the chance. His hands were already clawing at my throat in an effort to silence me; slender hands to suit his delicate frame, but with all the power and strength of fear behind them. If he fell into the clutches of the law, it would undoubtedly be a hanging matter; for whether he were responsible for Philip's death or no—and I had by no means made up my mind on that score—there were others who would certainly believe him guilty, and previous crimes which could probably be laid at his door. I thought it unlikely that Philip was the first of King Edward's messengers to have met a violent death through the machinations of Lancastrian agents.

With shaking fingers, I tore at his wrists and kneed him in the groin, but although Jeremiah Fletcher yelped, he refused to let go. When you are faced with the prospect of a rope around your neck, I imagine nothing else is of any importance and that terror deadens pain. Yet again that afternoon, the blood was drumming in my ears and there was a yellow mist before my eyes when help once more arrived, this time in the tardy shapes of Luke and John Groom. They had obviously been loath to believe me, but prudence had eventually won. With a shout compounded of anger and astonishment, they threw themselves upon my attacker and hauled him clear, bearing him roughly to the floor, where they both sat on his chest to pinion him down.

"B'lady, you'm right, maister," the groom said admiringly. " 'E were a thief, then! 'Ow did you know?"

I was still leaning against the bedchamber wall, gasping for breath, and all I could manage by way of answer was a froglike croak. Fortunately, I was for the moment spared any further efforts at conversation by the appearance not only of Alwyn Steward and James, but also of Janet Overy wielding a rolling-pin, the laundress brandishing the wooden stick used for removing linen from the tubs of boiling water, and the baker carrying the long-handled spatula with which he put in and took out the loaves from the ovens. Their various assistants, goggle-eyed at so much excitement in one day, brought up the rear.

"So," said Alwyn, "we have our thief and no doubt our murderer, too." He turned to me. "Do you know this man, Roger Chapman?" When I nodded, he gave a grunt of satisfaction. "And caught, seemingly, in the very act of trying to commit a second murder. You two men, and you, James, bring him along and we'll see him safely bestowed under lock and key until the Sheriff's officer arrives this evening." Relief at such a successful outcome, with no shred of blame attaching to any member of Sir Peveril's household, made the steward genial, and he led the way from the room with jaunty step and head held high. He could give a good account of events to his master on that gentleman's return; or as good an account as possible in the circumstances.

Janet put a hand beneath my elbow. "Come with me, lad. That throat of yours has taken more than its fair share of abuse this afternoon. But the same treatment as before will work miracles. You'll see."

I believed her, for she certainly seemed to know her herbs and remedies; and by the time she had once again completed her ministrations, I felt less pain and was able to make myself understood, although my voice was still ragged. Emerging into the courtyard, I learned that Jeremiah Fletcher, bound hand and foot, was securely locked in a small room in the chapel, with James, Luke and John Groom taking it in turns to guard him. Alwyn, who imparted this information, asked me to tell him all I knew about the prisoner; so, deciding that nothing would do now but the truth, I gave him the history of our ill-fated journey from my meeting with the Duke of Gloucester in Exeter to the present moment. Two things only I omitted; Silas Bywater's part in the story and any mention of the knotgrass.

I could see that Alwyn was impressed by the added stature which my version of events had given me. So, taking advantage of the fact, I asked if I might be allowed to see Jeremiah Fletcher alone for a few minutes.

"There are things which I have to ask him," I said,

managing to convey by my manner that these questions were of vital importance to the safety of the realm.

"We-ell . . ." The steward considered my request, then nodded briskly. "You have my permission, but make sure that Luke, who is standing watch at the moment, remains outside the door."

"If Fletcher is bound wrist and ankle, as you tell me, he can hardly be any danger to anyone."

"Nevertheless, I am not prepared to take chances. Please do as I ask." And the steward flung up an admonishing hand.

I gave my promise and was conducted into the gloom of the chapel which stood in one corner of the courtyard. The room where the prisoner was held was to the left of the altar, and was used by the chaplain to put on his vestments and say his prayers before Mass. A heavy oak door ensured his privacy at such times, and was equipped, for no good reason that I could see, with a stout lock and key. They were, however, proving useful at the moment, the key turned and removed from its resting-place, safely held in one of Luke's large brown hands. The other held a stout cudgel of only slightly smaller proportions than my own "Plymouth Cloak," which I recalled leaving propped up against one wall of the kitchen this morning, before sitting down to breakfast. The arrival of the sawyer's cart and the rest of the day's happenings had made me forget it was there. I must remember to move it out of Janet Overy's way.

The steward instructed Luke to let me into the robing-room and added sharply: "Leave the door unlocked while Master Chapman is inside and be alert to go to his assistance should he need you. After his departure, mind you lock the door again." Then he hurried fussily away.

Luke surveyed me curiously but asked no questions, merely doing as he was bidden. The key grated rustily in the lock as it was turned: obviously Sir Peveril's chaplain felt no need to secure himself against prying eyes. The door creaked a little on its hinges as Luke held it half open. I stepped inside.

The room was sparsely furnished, with a stone bench running the length of one wall and a chest in one corner. Daylight struggled to enter through a small window with leaded panes made of horn, and there was the customary bag, hanging from a nail, containing flint and tinder. A candle and candlestick, the former not yet lit, stood atop the chest. Jeremiah Fletcher, hands and feet tied together and a large bruise forming on his left cheek, was huddled at one end of the bench. I sat down at the other end and twisted round to face him. He eyed me balefully in return.

"And what do you want?"

"The truth, if that's not too much to ask." My voice was still hoarse and he grinned malevolently, plainly wishing that he could have finished his handiwork.

After a moment or two's consideration, he shrugged. "Why not? I'm a condemned man anyway, and have nothing more to lose. I've killed many men in my time, but ironically I shall be hanged for the murder I did not commit. Oh, I don't deny that I intended to take Philip Underdown's life—it's what I was being paid for—nor that I made two attempts to do so which went awry, once at the Abbey and again at the inn in Plymouth. But his death, when it came, was not by my hand. You can believe me or not as you please."

"I think I believe you," I answered. "But if you did not kill him, you might have seen who did."

He looked at me in astonishment, his eyebrows almost disappearing into his hair. "Why in heaven's name should you think that? When Master Underdown was murdered late last night—and that information I had from the landlord—I was asleep in my flea-infested bed in that equally flea-infested inn. Why should I be wandering the woods in the middle of the night?"

"For the same reason that you wandered Buckfast Abbey and the Plymouth streets. To do the bidding of your masters and prevent the King's messenger from reaching Brittany. You see, I am being perfectly frank. You followed Philip and me from Plymouth, arriving in Trenowth, according to Father Anselm, not long after us yesterday morning. And again according to the good father, you kept to your room at the inn all day, not even going downstairs for meals. You therefore had to spy out the land at night. I think you were abroad after dark and could have seen murder done."

Jeremiah Fletcher smiled thinly. "Very well, as you have guessed so much, I'll tell you that you are right, but only partly so. I was abroad last night with the intent, as you surmised, of spying out the land. But not until long after the murder had been committed. As I mounted the path towards the house, something, what exactly I cannot now say, but something attracted my attention to the river bank, where I found Philip Underdown's body, already stiffening and cold. It was a shock to discover that someone else had done my work for me, and so thoroughly. But to stab him, and then be forced to beat in the back of his head in order to kill him suggested that this obliging person was a novice at the task of murder."

"Did you search the body for the letter?" I asked.

His face clouded. "Ah, that letter! That has been the undoing of me." He shifted, trying to ease the constraint of his bonds. "Or perhaps I should rather say that you have been my nemesis. My masters certainly enjoined me to find and destroy the letter to Duke Francis if I could, but they did not know that Philip Underdown would be protected by a second man travelling with him. And indeed, until his arrival at Exeter, he was on his own, as is customary with royal messengers, who prefer to travel fast and unencumbered. But to have attacked him before his meeting with Duke Richard would have been useless. He did not then have the letter.''

I frowned. ''But how did your masters, as you call them, know that?''

He laughed. ''Who are you? *What* are you that you can ask such a question? Don't you know that the court of any country or state is riddled with spies? Even friends and allies spy upon each other. No noble lord worth his salt can afford but to have his paid informer in every other nobleman's household. Brother spies upon brother, father upon son. It's the way of the world. Wherever you go, France, Italy, Spain, you will find that to be the truth. The man whom Master Chaucer called the smiler with the knife under the cloak is everywhere.''

He was right. I was still very innocent in those days, unversed in man's cupidity, but I was learning fast. I repeated my question. ''Did you search the body?''

''Yes, of course I searched the body!'' He was growing tired of my interrogation and was in great discomfort. ''Later, as you know, I searched the bedchamber, but, as you also know, I was out of luck.''

''And how did you know which room to search?''

Jeremiah Fletcher groaned and leaned back heavily against the wall behind him. ''You have persistence, I'll grant you that! I didn't know. I saw a shutter and a window both open and a vine which was asking to be climbed. It was not until I was safely inside that I realized, by the articles of baggage strewn about, that it was yours and Master Underdown's. And now,'' he added wearily, ''if you have finished with me, leave me to my misery. I don't ask how you knew of my ruse to make a further search.

The carter is a garrulous as well as a gullible fool, and you fell in with him. Let us leave it at that." And he closed his eyes, his thin mouth set firmly, obviously determined to answer no more questions.

I was equally determined, however, to ask one more. "What does knotgrass mean to you?" I demanded.

He was sufficiently astonished to be betrayed into a reply.

"Knotgrass?" he said, opening his eyes. "It's a plant. A weed. Why should it mean anything to me?"

"No reason," I answered, rising. "But you're sure it has no special significance for you?"

"None whatsoever!" was the emphatic response.

I nodded and rapped on the door to let the guard know that I was about to come out, in case he thought Jeremiah Fletcher was trying to escape.

"All right, maister?" Luke asked me.

"I think your prisoner could do with food and water. I'll request Mistress Overy to see that he's fed."

I made my obeisance in front of the altar, then went outside. The hay had been unloaded, but the empty cart still stood in the middle of the courtyard. The carter had arrived to claim his property some time ago, or so I deduced from the fact that he and John Groom were seated on the bench outside the servants' quarters and were sipping ale together like lifelong friends. They were so deep in wide-eyed conversation that they did not even notice me as I crossed to the kitchen and made my plea on the prisoner's behalf to Mistress Overy. She, good soul, proved as sympathetic to his needs as I had expected her to be.

"Supper won't be long," she said, despatching one of the kitchen-maids to assemble a tray of food for Jeremiah Fletcher. "How's your throat? Can you eat?"

I sniffed the air. "If supper tastes as good as it smells, I'll force myself, however great the effort." She laughed and I went on: "Where's Silas Bywater? Have you seen him lately?"

She looked surprised. "Didn't you know? He's gone."

I stared at her, momentarily struck dumb with surprise. When eventually I found my voice, I asked: "How can he be gone? Who gave him permission? And why has the hue and cry not been raised? We were all to remain on the manor until the Sheriff's officer arrives."

"But matters stand differently now," Janet argued comfortably. "The murderer is under lock and key. You know him. He is the man, according to your story, who has already made two attempts on Master Underdown's life. Furthermore, he was taken in the act of trying to strangle you when you caught him stealing from your belongings. Silas Bywater wished to be on his way, and neither Alwyn nor I saw any reason to detain him longer. The Sergeant will have no need to question anyone except yourself." She turned to stir the contents of a pot hanging over the fire, adding curiously: "By the way, did this Jeremiah Fletcher find what he was looking for?"

I shook my head absently. "How long ago did Silas leave?"

She straightened her back, spoon in hand, and considered me doubtfully. "While you were questioning the prisoner in the chapel robe-room. Why? You are not thinking of going after him, surely?"

"There are things I still want to ask him. If I hurry, I may catch him up."

The housekeeper banged down the spoon on the table. "You and your questions!" she exclaimed with angry impatience. "What do they do except make more trouble for all of us? Why can't you accept the fact that the murderer is caught?"

I had been moving towards the kitchen door, but such was the vehemence of her tone that I paused and looked at her. For the first time, I wondered if Janet knew a little more about Philip's death than she had so far admitted. She had certainly been at great pains to persuade me that no one in or around Trenowth could have any knowledge of the murder. She had seized on the existence of Jeremiah Fletcher to convince me that there could be only one possible killer.

I hesitated, then decided against voicing my suspicions. If I were wrong, I should only incur her ill-will; if right, then my silence might eventually cause her to make a slip and point me in the direction of Philip's real murderer. I could not explain, even to myself, why I was so reluctant to accept what seemed so obvious to everyone else, that Jeremiah Fletcher, by his own admission a paid assassin, had successfully carried out his instructions. I suppose, looking back from the distance of years, the answer is that somewhere in my mind I already knew the identity of the killer. All the knowledge was there, with the exception of one vital piece, just waiting to be assembled in the proper order.

I heaved a great sigh and let my hands hang slack at my side. "You're right," I said meekly. "I've caused nothing but trouble for you and Isobel Warden and her husband. I'm sorry."

Relief at my capitulation made her genial in an instant. "That's all right, lad. You're not bred to this kind of thing, any more than the rest of us. And I must take some of the blame for encouraging your suspicions about Isobel in the first place. I thought myself that is was her Master Underdown had gone to meet, when all the time it was this Jeremiah Fletcher. He admits to the killing, does he?"

"To the first two attempts, yes, but denies the actual deed."

Janet snorted contemptuously. "Well, no one is going to believe that! Certainly not the Sheriff's officer. He's seen too many villains in his time to be taken in by such a story. And once he's heard from you the true version of events, he'll have no doubts whatsoever."

There I could agree with her. So neat a solution to the murder could not but appeal to one already hard pressed by the march of far more important happenings in the county. Cornishmen were arming themselves against the possibility, even the probability, of invasion and had little time to spare at present for other distractions. The Sergeant from Launceston Castle would be only too pleased to be able to report to Sir John Arundel the happy outcome of a case which, if left unsolved, might have brought down upon their heads much royal displeasure. So he would not be seeking any other solution to the mystery of who killed Philip Underdown. Jeremiah Fletcher's protestations of innocence, if he bothered to make any, would go unregarded. I recalled with a wry smile my earlier hope that I might be able to keep Philip's mission a secret from the Sheriff's officer. I had been too optimistic and too naïve, but at least the Queen's relatives were not involved, which would spare the King and his family much embarrassment. Looking back, I could see that I had been far too indiscreet, an innocent cast adrift in a world of intrigue. Had the Earl of Oxford's invasion of St. Michael's Mount never happened, and everything gone according to plan, it would not have mattered. Philip would have been in Brittany by now, the King's letter safely delivered, and I would have been on the road again, happy and contented.

Janet's voice interrupted my thoughts. "You have it safe? That letter that's caused all the trouble?"

If I fingered the left-hand edge of my jerkin, I could feel the stiff crackle of parchment between the leather and the lining, but I refrained from doing so and merely nodded.

"How long to supper?" I asked. "I'm hungry."

"When are you not?" she scolded gently. She dipped her spoon into the pot and tasted its contents. "A little while yet, but not too long. Go outside and get some air, but don't go far. And don't go chasing after Silas Bywater."

"I won't," I promised, suddenly feeling very weary. All that had happened that day, from the discovery of Philip's body to being nearly throttled twice, with all my exertions in between, was at last beginning to take its toll. What did it matter if the questions I wanted to ask Silas Bywater were never put to him? If a self-confessed murderer was convicted for a crime he hadn't committed? The energy which had coursed through me for the past hours was abruptly quenched. The only thing I wanted to do at the moment was to sleep. I stretched my arms until the bones cracked and yawned hugely.

Janet smiled. "You're worn out, lad. Go and lie down. I'll send one of the girls to call you when it's time for supper."

"I think I will," I said. "I've only just realized how tired I am. My throat still hurts as well." I glanced around me. "I left my cudgel here this morning, after breakfast. I thought

I left it by the door, but it's not there now. Either I was mistaken or somebody's moved it.''

"I did," Janet answered. "It's there, in that corner. I kept falling over it where it was." I noticed that she too was looking extremely tired and careworn. It had been a nightmarish day for all of us, and I was not surprised when she sat down at the kitchen table, fanning herself with her apron. She added: "Perhaps you'd better leave it here for the time being. The Sheriff's officer may wish to see it. We've laid the knife beside the body in the great hall, but it's possible he might wish to inspect both the weapons used. I'll see that no one takes it by mistake. I know how highly a man prizes his own particular sword or cudgel.''

I thanked her and got to my feet. My limbs felt like lead, as they so often do at the prospect of ease after great labours. Two little kitchen-maids, chatting and giggling to one another as they gathered together the bone-handled knives and stale trenchers of bread ready to lay the table for the evening meal, smiled shyly at me as I passed them. Their round, worshipping eyes told me that they regarded me as a hero who had unmasked a dangerous criminal, and I was too human not to find it pleasant, so I grinned and winked at them in return.

The courtyard was quiet now, the carter having departed with his wagon. John Groom was also invisible, but I could hear him whistling tunelessly inside the stable. A horse whinnied and I wondered if it were my rouncey or Philip's horse—now the property of Sir Peveril—who was missing his master. Luke was presumably still keeping watch inside the chapel, or else had been relieved by James. Either way, there was no sign of them. From the bakery, I could smell the sweet aroma of newly-baked bread which would be eaten at supper. Tomorrow there would be a new batch for the breakfast table. The laundry was empty now, the laundress and her assistants gone to their homes in the village, the linen dried and folded in the big baskets, await-ing the smoothing irons to get rid of the creases.

I crossed the great chamber and mounted the stairs to my room. Philip's and my belongings were still in a heap in the middle of his bed, just as they had been abandoned by Jeremiah Fletcher when I surprised him. Tonight I would pack everything into the saddle-bags, ready for my return to Plymouth on the morrow. But for now, I was too sleepy to do anything but let them lie where they were. I removed my jerkin, felt inside the lining, which I had never sewn up, to assure myself of the letter's safety, took off my boots and fell exhausted upon my truckle-bed. Mo-ments later, I was sleeping soundly.

And moments after that, I was awake again, sitting bolt upright and staring, slack-mouthed, before me. Then I swung my legs to the floor and began pulling on my boots with hands that shook, shrugged on my jerkin and was out of the room, down the stairs and across the courtyard to the stables almost before I knew it. I glanced furtively to-wards the kitchen to see if Janet were anywhere in sight and slipped inside the stables to find John Groom.

He was busy hauling the bales of fodder up the ladder to the hay-loft above and did not immediately hear me call his name. There were a number of stalls facing me as I entered, only two of which were occupied at present, by the cob and Philip's fleabitten grey. Of Sir Peveril's horses, one was being ridden to Launceston by the sawyer and the rest were presumably with him in London.

"John!" I exclaimed urgently, laying my hand on the ladder and shaking it as hard as I dared.

He paused in surprise and looked down, his face red with exertion. "Oh, it's you," he said. "Give me a hand with the rest of the bales, will you? The carter should by rights have done it, but he was anxious to be away. He was too ashamed to stay any longer after that stupid trick he played."

"I can't," I answered. "I must catch up with Silas Bywater. I need my horse now."

He grumbled and swore a good deal, but then his better nature overcame his ill-humour. He deposited his burden in the loft and descended once more to saddle the cob. He was a slow, thorough man and I had to curb my impatience, expecting every moment to hear Janet Overy beating spoon against skillet as a signal that supper was almost ready. At last, however, I was up and away, the rouncey frisking under me, delighted to renew our acquaintance. As I rode into the courtyard, Edgar Warden and his assistants appeared through the archway, having finished their day's work and eager now for their evening meal. The bailiff scowled at me as I passed, but offered no other sign of hostility, even managing to look a little ashamed of himself if the truth were told. I wondered if he and Colin and Ned had heard of the afternoon's events, if the news had as yet spread to all parts of the manor, or if they had still to be told of them, and what they would make of them when they knew.

But the thought was fleeting. I had too much else on my mind, not least the necessity of overtaking Silas Bywater and forcing him to tell me what it was that I needed to know. I felt sure that only he and one other held the key to the riddle of Philip Underdown's death. I knew beyond doubt now who the real murderer was, but was uncertain as to the reason. As I rode, I went back over the events of the past two days, since our arrival at Trenowth the previous morning, and began to see more clearly a pattern emerging. Things had been said and done which by themselves meant nothing, but put together started to form a picture. And I could go even further back, to one of my early conversations with Philip, and also to something which John Penryn had said.

"*There are always the cellars,*" he had told Philip. "*No ghosts. Just the best ale and wine this side of the Tavy.*"

Philip's own voice echoed through my head. "*I cannot bear to be cooped up. It frets me to be in a confined space for very long.*" And he had confessed to having nightmares about being chained up in the dark.

I stopped briefly in the village to make certain that Silas had not delayed his journey by a visit to the inn, but the landlord had not seen him. The landlord's wife, however, was more helpful.

"I met him just beyond the manor pale not an hour since, walking south. Said the murderer had been taken and he was free to return to Plymouth. Heading for the ferry, I reckon."

I thanked her and rode on, letting the rouncey have his head as much as I dared in view of the roughness of the tracks thereabouts and my inexpert horsemanship. I recognized very little of the country through which I passed, it having been dark when Philip and I traversed it, going in the opposite direction, in the pre-dawn hours of yesterday morning. The weather had cleared even more as the afternoon shadows lengthened, and there was now no sign of the morning's threatened storm. A very fine evening was promised and the distant hills were lost in a shimmering amber haze.

I seemed to have been riding for a long time, and was just beginning to worry lest Silas Bywater should for some reason or another have turned aside into one of the neighbouring villages, when, to my great relief, I emerged from a grove of trees and saw him four or five furrows' length ahead of me. I shouted to him to stop as loudly as I could and dug my heels into the cob's side, spurring him forward and soon overtaking my quarry.

Silas had turned in alarm at the sound of his name and was plainly considering the possibility of making a run for it. But in the end he decided to stand his ground and showed me a defiant face as I came abreast of him.

"What do you want?" he asked me in a surly voice. "Alwyn Steward and Mistress Overy gave me permission to go, now that you've caught the murderer." He looked suddenly suspicious. "The Sheriff's officer hasn't arrived yet, has he? It's not he who's told you to come after me? He doesn't wish me fetched back?"

I swung myself out of the saddle with a sigh of relief. In those days I was not a natural horseman. "You can be easy on that score," I reassured him. "There was no sign of either Thomas Sawyer or the Sergeant when I left Trenowth, although no doubt they'll be here before nightfall. No, I'm the one who wants a word with you. There is something I need to know which you can tell me, and as I intend to have the information one way or another, you might as well make it easy for yourself by answering my questions. I am, when all's said and done, much bigger than you."

He acknowledged this fact with an ill grace. "What is it you want to know?"

"There's a cottage over there," I pointed out, "and as I shall have missed my supper by the time I return to Trenowth, let's see if the goodwife will spare bread and cheese and small ale for two weary travellers. The horse, too, could do with a rest and some water."

Silas thawed a little with the realization that I was friendlier than he had at first supposed. "Very well," he agreed, falling into step beside me. "We might as well be comfortable, although I could tell you here and now what it is you want to know, because I can guess what it is you've come for."

It was nearly dark by the time I reached Trenowth manor house again. The gates of the compound still stood open and there was a bustle within which told me that the household was in imminent expectation of the Sergeant's arrival from Launceston. Cressets and torches had been lit in profusion, and Alwyn, hovering on the top step outside the great hall, staff of office in hand, had changed into his best furred gown. Even those servants who lived in the village and should long ago have gone to their homes still loitered around the courtyard, hoping to catch a glimpse of any drama that might unfold. Isobel and Edgar Warden were seated on the stone bench outside the servants' quarters, and John Groom came forward at once to take my rouncey, having seen me ride in from his position in the stable doorway. Only Janet Overy was missing, and a brief question elicited the fact that she was in the kitchen, putting the finishing touches to a meal especially prepared for the Sheriff's officer.

"You won't get anything," the groom informed me. "She was main put out that you weren't at supper."

I made no reply, but made my way to the kitchen, hoping against hope that I might find Janet alone. My prayers were answered, the two little maids having been sent outside in order to warn of the Sergeant's approach as soon as it was known. As I entered, Janet half-turned, thinking it to be one of the girls, but her face clouded when she saw who it was.

"And where have you been?" she demanded angrily. "You were supposed to be lying down on your bed."

I shut the kitchen door carefully behind me. "I went after Silas Bywater," I said.

Her voice became shrill. "Why? You promised me—"

"I know, and I'm sorry to have broken that promise. But I had to know, you see. I had to know why you killed Philip Underdown."

CHAPTER

19

 There was a protracted silence while I waited for her to deny the charge. But she didn't. Instead, she came forward and sat down heavily at the kitchen table.

"What made you suspect me in the first place?"

I swung my legs over the bench and sat opposite her. "Because you gave yourself away, twice. Earlier this afternoon, when I asked why you thought Philip Underdown chose to leave the bedchamber from an upper floor window rather than a lower, you answered that he might have been afraid of rousing me if he rose and dressed and went downstairs. But by putting me to sleep *outside the door*, he could climb down the vine without any such worry. I should have seen then what I saw later, that only from Philip himself could you have learned of that stratagem. I did not tell you and no one else knew of it."

She stared down at her hands which were clasped tightly together on the table in front of her. "And how did I give myself away the second time?"

"You were very tired, as I was. Your thoughts were muddled and confused by all the events of the day. You could no longer distinguish between what you knew and what you were supposed to know. You knew that it was my cudgel that had been used to bludgeon Philip Underdown to death when the attack with the knife had failed. Again, only he could have informed you that it was mine. Did you never pause to wonder why it wasn't found beside the body, or how it was brought back here?"

She raised her eyes then to look me full in the face, a slight frown furrowing her brows.

"Of course I wondered, but as you said a moment ago, there were things I was not supposed to know and therefore could not question."

"But you knew that I had discovered the corpse before Thomas Sawyer?"

"I did not know. I could not, without asking you for the truth. And I could not ask you without arousing your suspicions. But I guessed. You had realized that Master Underdown was absent from his bed long before you said you did. You went after him and found him dead. You also found that he had taken your cudgel and that it had been used to kill him. You naturally brought it away to save yourself from being suspected of the crime." I nodded and she continued: "Don't think I blame you, lad. Any sensible man would have done the same." She heaved a sigh of self-reproach. "And then, foolishly, I betrayed myself. I was desperately tired and unable to think clearly any longer. I prayed to God you would not notice my error, but I knew He would not hear me. What right have I to His protection? I have taken the life of a fellow creature." She put her hands over her eyes for a moment, then withdrew them. "The earlier mistake I admit I did not notice. You have a sharp ear and brain."

I shook my head. "You give me greater credit than is my

due. It escaped my notice, also, at the time. Even your second error did not immediately strike me, but took a little while to penetrate my mind. If it is any consolation to you, however, I had already begun to suspect you knew more about the murder than you admitted to."

"Why?" Janet wanted to know. "Where did I go wrong?"

I shrugged. "There was no one particular thing. But when I thought about it, your behaviour was full of contradictions. First, you said no one could leave the compound at night because the gates were locked. Then you told me that anyone, if he or she so wished, could get out of the lower storey windows. Again, you played on my belief that Philip must have gone to meet Isobel Warden, and encouraged my conviction that her husband was a very jealous man, until your conscience began to bother you. After that, you did your very best to convince me that Jeremy Fletcher was the murderer—as undoubtedly he would have been had he ever been given another chance. You also tried to dissuade me from making any further inquiries. And it was you, I fancy, rather than Alwyn Steward, who was anxious to let Silas Bywater go before I questioned him too closely about the meaning of knotgrass. With your knowledge of herbs and medicinal plants, I think you already know its deadly properties."

There was another silence before she answered quietly: "Yes, I know them." She drew a painful breath. "Were there any other mistakes I made?"

"They weren't truly mistakes, only some small things which by themselves meant nothing, but added to the rest had some significance. You said you had lost your son, but you did not say that he was dead. It was natural in me to assume so, but I repeat, you did not say so. And this afternoon, when you were attending to my hurts, you told me you were fond of me, adding: "My son should have looked like you . . ." Not "would," meaning had he lived, but "should," a word suggesting that he ought to resemble me, but that some terrible mishap had befallen him. And finally, on your own admission, the apportioning of rooms to visitors is your responsibility in Lady Trenowth's absence. At first I thought it merely fortuitous that Philip and I had been allotted the bedchamber with the vine outside the window. But you had recognized Philip as soon as you saw us both in the courtyard. I believe it was in that moment that the idea of taking revenge on him sprang into your mind. You had formed no clear plan, except to feel that a second means of egress from the room could only prove of value. Am I right?"

Janet's level gaze met mine. "I thought you a bright young man when I first set eyes on you, but that was an injustice. I see now that you are even cleverer than I suspected." She got up, went to the kitchen door, opened it and asked something of one of the maids. When she returned to her seat at the table, she said: "There is as yet no sight of the Sheriff's officer and Thomas Sawyer, so tell me what you found out from Silas Bywater."

"Let me go back further," I said, "to my first meeting with Philip Underdown last Thursday." Was it indeed only five days ago since that meeting? It seemed like a lifetime away. "He told me then, without shame or apology, of his life before becoming a royal messenger; that he had been a trader of, among other commodities, human flesh; unfortunate, dwarfish children who would never grow to full height and whose parents were anxious to be rid of them, or who saw them as the means of a little easily-come-by wealth. I wondered how he and his brother could find enough such children to make money at the trade, and he said that there were always ways and means if one knew them. At the time, I had no notion what he meant."

"But you do now?"

"Yes. Silas Bywater told me. My mother, God rest her soul, was wrong, but not so very wrong, in her belief that knotgrass contains a poison which will kill you."

"No," Janet answered in a voice which was almost inaudible. "Not so very wrong. An infusion of knotgrass and daisies, if taken in sufficient quantities, stunts children's growth, making them dwarfish. I have no doubt that that is what happened to my son after he was stolen from me, any more than I have any doubt who was responsible. I have listened to you, and now I ask you to listen to me while I tell you my side of the story."

Janet Overy had been a widow for, she thought, about five years when her son disappeared. As she had told us, her husband had been drowned at sea a week before young Hugh was born. A fisherman, the only thing of value he owned, his boat, had gone down with him, and his wife and child had been left destitute. Janet's hard and unremitting work as a seamstress had saved them both from starving, but she had grudged neither time nor labour as long as her beautiful son wanted for anything that she could possibly give him.

She had, from time to time, gone into Plymouth to buy those things which she was unable to grow or raise in her small patch of garden, and it was on one of these occasions that she had first seen Philip Underdown and his brother.

"They were difficult men to miss," she said. "Bold, handsome, dark, striding about the wharves as if they owned them, overseeing the loading of their ship, the *Speedwell*. Then I would not see them for a year or more, and I learned that they traded out of other ports. Bristol and London. But they always turned up again eventually."

She knew nothing about the two brothers other than what she saw and was always too busy to stop and gossip, being acquainted with very few people in the city. She had no idea of the kind of merchandise the *Speedwell* carried, nor would she have thought much of it, apart from a natural repulsion, if she had. Her little Hugh was a lovely child, his young body healthy and perfectly formed, with none of the deformities which so often, and so unhappily, afflicted other children.

And then, on a fine, sunny day not long after his fifth birthday, he disappeared. Janet had been busy with her sewing and had shooed her son outdoors to play, where he would not be continually under her feet. When she went to call him for supper an hour or so later, there was no sign of him anywhere. She had called and searched until it grew dark, but never found him. The following morning, as soon as it was light, she roused her neighbours to join in the hunt, but to no avail. Hugh had vanished.

The distraught mother had gone south as far as Plymouth and north to Tavistock, but all the time hope of discovering her child was fading. And then one day she had fallen in with an old, lame beggar who recollected seeing two men in the vicinity of Janet's village about the time of Hugh's disappearance.

"He remembered because it was two weeks after Easter and the hocking had begun. He saw two men on horseback, one of them with a fair-haired boy held before him in the saddle. The child was crying bitterly and the man silenced him with a blow."

The beggar's description of the two men immediately brought Philip Underdown and his brother to mind and Janet set out once again for Plymouth. When she got there, however, she found that the *Speedwell* had set sail for Genoa some weeks earlier with both men and their cargo aboard. It was then, asking among the freight-loaders of the Sutton harbour quayside, that she had learned of their trade in dwarfs. But she had dismissed the intelligence as of no interest to her. It was not until years later, when she had found sanctuary as housekeeper at Trenowth Manor and in its tranquillity regained a little of her peace of mind, that she learned, quite by chance from a mendicant friar, of the fate which had probably befallen her child.

"He told me," Janet said, "of cases he had known where, because the demand among the nobility of every country was now so great for dwarf attendants, and the supply of truly stunted boys and men insufficient, the traders stole healthy children who were chained up for months, sometimes for more than a year, in dark cellars, half-starved and forced to drink copious infusions of knotgrass and daisies, which inhibited their natural growth. He knew Plymouth, and I asked him if he had ever heard such a thing whispered about the masters of the *Speedwell*. He admitted reluctantly that he had, although nothing had ever been proved against either of the Underdown brothers. And if they did steal children, where did they keep them?"

"The cellars of the Turk's Head," I interrupted with conviction. "That was where they kept them. And no doubt there were inns and landlords in London and Bristol equally willing to oblige for a share in the profits."

It was small wonder, I reflected, that inns and ale-houses had such a bad reputation when often it was so richly deserved; unsurprising that, twice-yearly at the manorial courts, villagers were asked to name those of their number who "haunted taverns." I recalled an inn I had known in London two years previously, and shivered at the recollection.

After the friar had left, Janet had visited Plymouth again, only to learn that the younger of the two Underdowns was dead and no one knew what had become of the elder. The only thing certain was that he no longer traded from the city.

"I had to force myself to forget him and his brother. No

doubt remained in my mind that they were indeed the men who had taken away my son, nor about what they had done to him. But one of them was beyond my reach in Hell, and the other would one day follow him. That was my consolation. And then . . ."

"And then, yesterday morning, you saw him standing in the courtyard, self-satisfied and prosperous. It was more than you could stomach."

Janet nodded. "I made up my mind in that very first moment that I was going to kill him. The rest you know."

"You persuaded him to meet you, very late at night, down by the river."

She smiled. "I didn't have to persuade him. He played straight into my hands. I had made it plain to him at breakfast that I liked him, and whatever you might think, lad, I'm neither so old nor so decrepit that a man can't fancy me." I blushed that she should have read my mind so easily. "He was a man who liked women, that was obvious to someone as experienced as I am, and would need entertainment if he were to remain at Trenowth for any length of time. I did not think he would bother Isobel. He had taken Edgar's measure and Philip Underdown was a man who treasured the wholeness of his skin. So I was not surprised when he appeared in the kitchen yesterday morning—"

"Having rid himself of me with the story that he had seen from the bedchamber window someone lurking in the trees."

"—put his arm about my waist and kissed me. I put up a little show of indignation for the sake of the girls, then sent them on errands to other parts of the house. Master Underdown and I drank ale together and soon came to an understanding—or so he thought. He was somewhat nonplussed by my insistence on meeting him outside the house instead of in the comfort of my room, but I told him I dared not risk discovery as I was being courted by Alwyn.

He accepted the lie without further question, and also submitted to my request that we each make our separate way to the trysting-place in case, by ill chance, we were seen. I could let myself out by the wicket gate because I hold the key, but I suggested that, unless he felt himself to be too old or unfit, he climb out of the window by the vine. There would then be no risk of both of us being spotted crossing the courtyard by some sleepless soul."

"And of course he accepted this challenge to his manhood."

"Of course, as I had known he would." Janet raised her hands and covered her eyes for a moment. When she removed them, she looked almost as if she might swoon. "I never thought it would be so difficult to kill a man. I had taken one of the kitchen knives with me, carefully sharpened, and imagined that I had only to plunge it into his breast to strike him dead. But it wasn't like that at all. He was waiting for me when I arrived and immediately embraced me and kissed my lips. God help me, I even felt the stirrings of response! I tried to push him away, but he kept nuzzling my hair, which I had left uncovered and unbound, telling me how clever he had been in getting you to sleep outside the bedchamber door. I asked why he had brought a cudgel with him, and he answered that he felt safer roaming around in the dark if he had protection against thieves and footpads. I know now that he had other enemies to fear."

"And he told you it was mine?"

"The cudgel? He must have done, or I shouldn't have known. But I don't recall his actual words. I was bracing myself to strike. I managed at last to free myself from his arms, brought the knife out of my pocket and plunged it into his breast." She made a sound which was half sob, half laugh. "The look of astonishment on his face was ludicrous. He could not believe what was happening. There was no reason that he knew of why I should wish to kill him. He fell to his knees, trying to pull out the knife which had gone in up to the haft. Blood was trickling from the side of his mouth, but he was still alive. In horror, I picked up the cudgel—your cudgel—which he had placed on the ground and began hitting him with it, again and again, on the back of the head.'' She shuddered. ''I was covered with blood. It was horrible, but all I could think of was my little boy, robbed of his mother and his proper life, turned into a dwarf for the pleasure of some Milanese or Florentine nobleman. Eventually, when I was finally satisfied that Philip Underdown was dead, I threw down the cudgel and ran back here as fast as I could. You'll find the blood-stained dress at the bottom of the robe-chest in my room, hidden under my other clothes.'' We stared at one another across the table. ''So now you know what really happened,'' she said at last. ''What do you intend to do?''

''I don't know,'' I answered slowly. ''I can't find it in my heart to blame you. In your place, I think I would have done the same.''

''But you don't think it fair to let someone else, not even a self-confessed murderer, take the blame for something he did not do?''

A shout came from the courtyard and there was the sudden bustle of an arrival. Thomas Sawyer had returned with the Sheriff's officer. It was time to go out and welcome them and tell them what I knew.

''Was it you,'' I asked, ''who put the bunch of daisies and the knotgrass in our bedchamber?''

Janet got to her feet, smoothing down her skirt. ''Yes. I don't really know why I did it, except to remind him of what he had done, of the lives he had broken, never to be mended. But you didn't let him see them. Perhaps if you had, at the very end, he might have understood why he was killed.''

EPILOGUE

In all the years between then and now, half a century which has seen so much change and made us more cynical in our way of thinking, I have often wondered if I did right to let Janet Overy go free and escape the consequences of her deed. And I have never found the answer. It still must be a crime in the eyes of God to let another person suffer for your wrongdoing, even if that person is evil and would have suffered the full penalty of the law for other misdeeds. Yet I could not bring myself even then to denounce her for what she did to Philip Underdown; and since I have held my own children in my arms and watched them grow to sturdy man- and womanhood, I have never regretted my decision for an instant. How I shall fare on the Day of Judgement, when I stand at last before the Creator of us all, the Being who is privy to the secrets of everyone's heart, I do not know. Shall I be judged more harshly for my collusion in covering up the truth or for my lack of repentance? Only God can decide.

I suppose I can argue that at least I told the Sheriff's officer no lies. I simply did not tell him all the truth. I made no accusation against Jeremiah Fletcher except to repeat his admission that he had twice tried to take Philip's life during the past five days, and that he was a self-confessed agent for the enemies of the King; a traitor as well as a murderer. But it was not the Sergeant's fault that he looked no further for the slayer of a royal messenger who was carrying an important letter to the Duke of Brittany.

Janet and I watched in silence the following morning as Jeremiah Fletcher was led away in chains. In fact we spoke very little, avoiding each other's company, after that conversation in the kitchen. We said a brief goodbye before I returned to Plymouth, taking with me my borrowed rouncey, but leaving Philip's fleabitten grey to enjoy his new home. The Sheriff's officer had promised to send a messenger to Simon Whitehead at Falmouth, but gave his approval to my plan to go myself to Brittany if I had heard nothing to the contrary by the time the *Falcon* arrived in Sutton harbour.

What is there left to say of this adventure, except that I went to Brittany and delivered King Edward's letter to Duke Francis in person? It was the first time I had ever left these shores, and the first time I ever saw that Lesser Britain, with whose inhabitants we share a common heritage, and of which, in ancient times, this island was known as the Greater part. When I returned to Plymouth several weeks later, I found my rouncey patiently waiting for me at the stables where I had left him, and together we made our way back to Exeter and the Bishop's Palace. I made my report to His Grace, said farewell to the horse, picked up my pack and thankfully resumed my life on the open road.

I heard many months later, by roundabout ways, that the Duke of Gloucester's men had come searching for me in Exeter two weeks after I left, and that the Duke was angry with Bishop John Bothe for letting me go unrewarded. But in those far-off days I was young and footloose and fancy-free, wanting nothing but my freedom. The life I had chosen had its hardships and pitfalls, but I answered to no man, owed no one anything but myself.

As for the success of my mission, everyone knows now that Duke Francis stayed his hand, offering no succour to the beleaguered Earl of Oxford on St. Michael's Mount. After that first desperate assault on the fortress, when Sir John Arundel and so many of his troops were slain in the sand at the foot of the main stairway, the attacks dwindled in number until, finally, the new sheriff, Sir John Fortescue, was content to blockade the Mount by land and sea, eventually starving the Earl and his men into submission the following February. Oxford was sent to Calais where he spent the next nine years as a prisoner in Hammes Castle. Henry Tudor and his Uncle Jasper remained as "guests" in Brittany.

I never saw Janet Overy again, but during one of my visits to that part of the country I was told by someone who had known her that she had left Trenowth Manor quite suddenly to go on pilgrimage to Rome, and had never returned. Sometimes she haunts my dreams; a lost, melancholy ghost, wandering from one Italian city to another, searching, endlessly searching, for a poor maimed and stunted man who was once her beautiful child. And I wake with the tears running down my face, wishing that Philip Underdown and I had never set foot in Trenowth; that she had been left to eke out her broken life in peace.

KATE SEDLEY introduced Roger the Chapman, her fifteenth-century peddler-cum-amateur-detective, to critical acclaim in *Death and the Chapman*. With *The Plymouth Cloak*, she makes a welcome return to her richly detailed setting and most unusual and charming sleuth. A student of Anglo-Saxon and medieval history, Sedley lives in England.

STILL WATERS and COLD FEET
by Kerry Tucker

Take off on two crime-filled adventures with fiesty photo-journalist and amateur sleuth Libby Kincaid and find out why the *Cleveland Plain Dealer* says "Kerry Tucker is going to be an important part of the mystery scene. She writes like a champ." In STILL WATERS, Libby travels to her hometown of Darby, Ohio to uncover the truth behind the mysterious death of her brother. In COLD FEET, Libby combs New York's sweltering summer streets to find a killer.